TRAVELS WITH

Also by Menna Gallie, published by Honno:

The Small Mine
Strike for a Kingdom
You're Welcome to Ulster

TRAVELS WITH A DUCHESS

by

MENNA GALLIE

*With an introduction
by
Angela V. John*

HONNO CLASSICS

Angela V. John is an Honorary Professor of History at Aberystwyth University. Her most recent book is *Evelyn Sharp: Rebel Woman 1869–1955* (Manchester University Press, 2009). She is currently working on a biography of Lady Rhondda. She knew Menna Gallie well and has written the introductions for two other reprints of her novels, *You're Welcome to Ulster* and *Strike for a Kingdom*, also published by Honno Press.

Published by Honno
'Ailsa Craig', Heol y Cawl, Dinas Powys,
South Glamorgan, Wales, CF64 4AH.

1 2 3 4 5 6 7 8 9 10

First published in England by Victor Gollancz Ltd., in 1968
First published by Honno in 1996
This edition © Honno, 2011

© Estate of Menna Gallie, 1968
© Introduction Angela V. John, 1996

A catalogue record for this book is available from
the British Library.

Published with the financial support of the
Welsh Books Council.

ISBN 978-1-906784-22-5

Cover photograph © Image Source/Getty Images
Cover design: Graham Preston
Printed in Wales by Gomer Press

Foreword

In the summer of 1926 Menna Humphreys was six. Unlike most of her friends in the Swansea Valley village of Ystradgynlais, her father was not a collier on strike but a craftsman. Each Sunday he ritualistically divided a bar of chocolate between his three daughters, Nansi, Pegi and Menna, meticulously measuring out their portions with his carpenter's ruler. One particular week, Menna stood outside her front door to savour her treat on her own. Just as she was smoothing out the empty wrapper, a little girl who had been intently watching her from a distance came up and whispered, 'Can I have the smell of the paper?' In later years Menna Gallie would claim that it was this pitiful request which prompted her to write *Strike for a Kingdom*, her first novel. Whether or not this was so – she was a consummate teller of stories who could always transform retrospectively even the most humdrum event into a drama – the effect of the General Strike on her local community, and thus on the young Menna Humprheys, was a lasting one.

Menna Gallie was from a Welsh-speaking, socialist background. Her father was a north-Walian but her mother was local, one of nine children, eight of whom lived within two miles of each other. In this extended family 'aunts stood around us like the Druids' stones'. When the wireless came, her eldest aunt would elect to listen to the fatstock prices in Welsh rather than hear even a religious service in English. Menna Gallie's maternal grandfather, a colliery checkweighman who also ran a small farm, had helped found the Labour Representation Committee in south Wales. Keir Hardie had stayed at her grandparents' house and her

monoglot grandmother proudly claimed to have two sentences of English: 'I *like* ice-cream' and 'Keir Hardie called
me Comrade'. Menna's mother became secretary of the
local women's section of the Labour Party though her roots
lay in the Independent Labour Party. The Humphreys children sang Welsh hymns at the Congregational chapel and
eisteddfodau but they also sang 'God Save the People' at
home. Menna remained a lifelong Labour Party activist,
maintaining that she was 'not much of an "-ist" except that
I'm a Socialist'.

Growing up in Ystradgynlais and Creunant (in the Dulais
valley), then studying for an English degree at Swansea
University, it is hardly surprising that Menna Gallie set *Strike
for a Kingdom* (1959) in a Welsh mining village which she
called Cilhendre. A sequel, her third novel, *The Small Mine*
(1962), was set at a time when the new National Coal Board
mines coexisted cheek-by-jowl with the many small, private
drift mines. Yet, critical of the 'sociology and sentimentality'
to which mining communities were continually subjected,
she challenged (though also sometimes unconsciously rein-
forced) the stereotypical imagery of the mining village.
However, only two of her six novels were actually set in the
Valleys communities she knew best even though two others
were about Welsh characters and her last novel, as yet published only in America, *In These Promiscuous Parts* (1986),
is located in north Pembrokeshire where she spent her last
years (for Trenewydd read Newport/Trefdraeth). She also
wrote a booklet about the folklore of this part of
Pembrokeshire, *Little England's Other Half* (1974). In 1973
her translation of Caradog Prichard's sombre novel *Un Nos
Ola Leuad* appeared, entitled *Full Moon*.

Her first novel was hidden away for two years in a drawer
before it saw the light of day. When she was eventually persuaded to retrieve it, the manuscript was immediately accepted by the respected left-wing publisher Victor Gollancz.

Pronounced 'fresh and beguiling' by the *Times Literary Supplement*, it was well reviewed and Gollancz went on to publish five of her six novels. Her fiction was also published in America (where there is even a Menna Gallie Archive). There she received greater acclaim than in the UK, her initial popularity perhaps prompted in part by comparisons her early critics made with the work of Dylan Thomas. *Strike for a Kingdom* was declared to be 'a poet's novel' despite being in part a detective story.

Neither of Menna Gallie's Cilhendre stories was actually written in Wales. Here she was creating what seems to have become a pattern for her fiction: experiencing a community at first-hand but delaying writing about it until her thoughts had gestated for some time and she had moved on to a new place. Thus *Strike for a Kingdom* was actually written in Ulster, as was her second novel, *Man's Desiring* (1960). In 1940 she had married, just four days before he went off to the army, a philosophy lecturer at Swansea, a Scot called Bryce Gallie. *Man's Desiring*, with hints of Kingsley Amis's better-known *Lucky Jim*, concerns a Welsh working-class lad who tries to make it at an English university. It is based on the time the Gallies spent at Keele, where Bryce Gallie was appointed the first Professor of Philosophy.

Her tragi-comedy, *You're Welcome to Ulster!* (1970) was written in Cambridge. The experience of being a don's wife at Peterhouse (Gallie held the Chair of Political Science at Cambridge between 1967 and 1978) was not one Menna Gallie relished. She had far preferred the years in Northern Ireland where her son and daughter had grown up. Significantly, there is no novel about the Cambridge years. Yet in *Travels with a Duchess* (1968) she describes how the academic wife tends to look a decade older than her husband, feeling the strain of being 'the little handmaiden, helpmate, slave, they get to look like caricatures of denial', Cambridge brought out most keenly her innate defence of women's rights in the face of institutional denial – although Menna Gallie was always cautious about the label 'feminist'.

Travels with a Duchess has no real duchess but an Irishwoman who could assume the air of a 'Viennese-waltz sort of duchess'. Nor is it about a rugged trek with a donkey. Instead we are plunged into that new and liberating experience of the sixties, the package holiday. And, given Menna Gallie's politics, it's a carefully chosen destination: Dubrovnik in Tito's Yugoslavia. Its origins lay in two visits the author made personally to that country in the mid-1960s. One was as a delegate for Northern Ireland at a conference of PEN (the International Association of Poets, Playwrights, Editors, Essayists and Novelists). The other was a fortnight in Dubrovnik, taken by the writer after an illness. Her travelling companion was a close woman friend from Northern Ireland who had recently had twins in her mid-forties. As in the story, Menna's luggage never arrived at the resort.

The novel opens in Cardiff where Innes Gibson, the narrator, is a schoolteacher, menopausal and badly needing a break from teaching unacademically-gifted pubescent boys. Menna Gallie had herself taught for two years at a Belfast boys' school, finding equally challenging both of her charges – the sixth-formers and those who used, unfortunately, to be labelled 'ESN'.

The decision to make Innes unexpectedly travel on her own, before she encounters her future room-mate, the eponymous duchess and beautiful mother of six, Joan Maguire, enables Menna Gallie to explore the difficulties and fears a married woman faced in such a situation. At London Airport she finds the barmen 'nasty and young and superior and I was a solitary woman'. People wouldn't believe that a woman might choose to be on her own and there were bureaucratic indignities too. Having a joint passport, Innes is peremptorily informed that a wife can't travel alone; after all, there is no assurance that she is using the passport with her husband's consent. Innes feels provincial and inadequate. There is a hilarious scene in the 'Ladies' where, to her mortification, she discovers that her red suede suit has moulted. Not only has it spread like measles all over her cream blouse but it has also infected one of the immaculate '*Vogue* types' who is now covered in lumpy flecks.

Bereft of all her own clothes bar the offending suit, which she can hardly wear in the heat of Dubrovnik, Innes borrows clothes and in the process discards some of her old inhibitions. After a quarter of a century as the wife of a middle-class professional (who does not think to describe herself thus, despite her own job) and armed with her sixteen words of Serbo-Croat, she and Joan revel in the sun and slivovitz and learn that every local man seems to want 'cinque minuti', even amongst the icons: '"Ych y fi", with three teeth and dribbles as well, no doubt.'

The American paperback describes the novel as 'torrid, bawdy, razor-sharp', the jacket depicting a tall, sophisticated woman in a slinky dress with a *svelte* young man eyeing her from behind. Yet the essence of the tale lies in the camaraderie between the two women and their negotiation of their new-found, albeit temporary, freedom. It is a woman's novel, luxuriating in its frankness, and, for Innes and Joan, it is a 'holiday romance' which they have created together, one which can never exist back home.

For today's reader, Yugoslavia has become history and the corner of the world which formed an escape for the two women is the scene of brutal conflict. There is now an especial poignancy in the novel's suicidal figure who explains his difference from his wife by stressing that he is a Bosnian boy. Finely tuned by her upbringing to the meanings of ethnic identity and the potential destruction and romanticization of communities through tourism, we catch a glimpse of the serious side of Menna Gallie's writing (always there just below the surface) in her depiction of a day trip to Mostar, the dignity of the gypsy woman, and the author's passionate hatred of anyone who patronizes.

Yet this book, with its Kinsey Report and Krafft-Ebing references, must have seemed shocking to some when first published. Britain of the 1960s has been liberally re-invented as 'swinging' and promiscuous for all, ignoring the fact that such labels can at best only be applied to the last few years of the decade and then only for a limited number of people and places, whilst much of this was not necessarily progressive for women. *Travels'* avowal of woman's sexuality, glorying in physicality from a woman's viewpoint, is designed to shock, yet was written before the development of the modern British women's movement. What makes Innes feel guilty is not the fact that she sleeps with a virtual stranger but her belated discovery that he is a racist. Here is the outrage.

The period revered youth culture. Yet the opening of *Travels* makes it clear that this will be no story of students and 'flower power': 'When you're a woman about the late forty mark and time's winged chariot is up to its unmannerly chunterings at the back door, you let yourself get these terrible despairings.' The story is about women who fear ageing yet who show that it does not have to defeat them.

This is the first of Menna Gallie's novels to be reprinted. Some belated recognition of the force of her writing is now becoming evident. In the last few years she has been the subject of several articles (for example, Angela Fish, 'Flight-deck of experience', *New Welsh Review*, no. 18, Autumn 1992; Aled Rhys William, 'Nofelydd y Cymoedd Glo', *Barn*, no. 22, 1994) whilst Hywel Francis has recently described her and Elaine Morgan as Wales's 'two most prominent feminist writers' (*New Welsh Review*, no. 26, Autumn, 1994). Had she still been alive, Menna Gallie would probably have questioned that adjective. In a talk she gave at Onllwyn Miners' Welfare Hall in 1985 (five years before her death at the age of seventy) to an audience of miners' wives and academics interested in Welsh women's history, she carefully denied that she was a feminist. White-haired and crippled with arthritis, she looked deceptively frail. Yet she always delighted in provoking, in shocking, in protesting. She spoke for over an hour, dressed in a red suit of course, telling stories about her life, her practice and attitudes, palpably belying her verbal protestations.

Since this Introduction was written it has been discovered that even though Menna Gallie celebrated 17 March 1920 as her date of birth, she was in fact born on 18 March 1919.

Angela V. John, Newport, Pembs., Summer 1996
With thanks to Professor Bryce Gallie and Professor Hywel Francis

CHAPTER 1

When you're a woman around the late forty mark and time's winged chariot is up to its usual unmannerly chunterings at the back door, you let yourself get these terrible despairings. It's not so much a positive, black suicidal thing, not with me, anyway, but a feeling of cancellation; you feel you epitomize the notion of negation. You've been nothing, done nothing, deserve nothing. Guilts corrode you, you feel wary and tight and unloving, and you're alone with it.

One of the things you feel worst about is old sex, especially if you've exulted in it and it's been a marvellous communicator and you think it's nearly over. At your age you feel you might even begin to count how many times you'll have it again. You feel like an over-dried piece of washed linen that may have to wait in vain for the benison of a hot iron and a sprinkling of damp to take out the crimp and the creases.

You read all this stuff about sleeping around, and you take a sly, furtive peep at the Kinsey Report and Krafft-Ebing, and your eyes pop and it all sets you wondering, and if you feel wicked you've got this excuse they call pre-menopausal instability.

It's all this talk about it that does the harm; if they left you alone, you'd never have. Probably. Take this friend of mine, for example. She was devoted to her husband, minded him like a child and loved him well, but they got into a sort of routine in bed and he got gradually bored with preliminaries and she was a nice, modest girl and didn't like to say how much she enjoyed the preliminaries. It's funny what you can't say to husbands because they are husbands.

Anyway, she met this chap at a party one night when she wasn't speaking to her husband – some row or other about

the kids – and for spite she went out and sat in this car with
this fellow.

He was interested in the preliminaries all right. Oh, my
goodness, he was, but in the back of a small car you can't do
much in the way of a follow-up so she went home and they
made it up and she never had it so good. And that's how she
came to have a lover and didn't have a conscience about it at
all, because she claimed she needed the two of them, had a
right to the two of them. Between the two it was great and
anyway made her a much nicer wife.

I used to feel a bit sorry for the boy friend but she claims
he's never realised his function and feels the frustrations of
their affair are his fault because he has this game knee and
can't do gymnastics in the back of a car; she refuses to risk
being seen with him anywhere else and anyway, what can he
expect with a lame leg? But if she hadn't read these novels
and articles and things she wouldn't have got this notion
about her rights and all that jazz.

I'm sure I'd have stopped at the wondering if I hadn't
gone on that holiday last summer, but I went and now I've
stopped wondering.

I was teaching part-time in a Boys' Secondary Modern
and I'd have had no problems there if they'd let me spend all
my time with the big boys. I'm good with big boys because
I don't adjust to them, I mean I talk to them the way I talk to
professors, consultants, hoover men, men reading the meter,
cats, dogs, hens. In the sixth form they liked it that I talked
like one of the boys, for a female in a boys' school I think it's
the only way you can hope to teach, but when it's the educationally sub-normals you have a few problems.

In my usual way, I was treating them as my equals, which
of course they're not. Good heavens, no! Educationally sub-
normal boys of fourteen to fifteen have got a class of genius
for persecution, for example, that puts the Inquisition out of
the history. It wasn't that they didn't like me; no, I'm sure

they were fond of me in their fashion, they liked the paint and powder smell of me and the curve of my breasts and were amused by my funny-looking little monkey-face and they always expected me to laugh, to share their delight at my discomfiture.

The nasty thing was, though, that I was repelled by them; not only by the boy smell of them, like a dirty old plimsoll left in a cupboard; you get used to that in a boys' school and stop gagging even after a few hours as long as you stop working out the ingredients of the smell. That's fatal, that is, feet, pee, sweat, excreta, old clothes, pubescence, no, you just have to take it and gulp.

It wasn't the smell that put me off, it was more an aesthetic insult to my notion of man, I think. Their pubescence was so strident, so powerful and painful, so gauche and unpretty, their swelling noses, thickening lips and all that, undirected, reaching, bursting gush of impending sex, it was overwhelming and embarrassing as the zoo on a sunny afternoon.

Anyway, they drove me up the wall. I couldn't even keep them quiet enough for the man next door to hear himself bawl at his own class. Oh, it was shameful, it really was; they used to have these spitting competitions for one thing. I never did understand the sentence "I spit upon you" because when I spit the spit falls down, straight, but this old form 3B had learned how to make their spit defeat gravity and could literally spit in your eye. Not my eye, mind, only each others, and spit in the eye isn't pretty, you know. I should have been firm the first time I saw this phenomenon, but scientific curiosity got the better of my judgement and I looked interested and of course that tore it. Demonstrations then all over the class and the headmaster walks in. Jesus!

Then there was the day when they were acting out that rather nasty poem which children love, The Highwayman. The sub-normals love acting things out and they were having the time of their lives, with me tied up as the landlord's

black-eyed daughter and Robinson highway-manning in my
master's gown. You know the bit that goes "King George's
men came marching, marching, marching", well they were
marching a deafening treat and then, suddenly, everyone
burst out singing. But it wasn't like Sassoon – they all burst
out singing "Marching, marching, marching as to war, with
the cross of Jesus, going on before". Big, breaking, tuneless
voices, singing all the verses; the school rocking, chalk
bouncing in that ridge under the blackboard and the marching, round and round and round and me tied up and impotent,
and masters from the three nearest class-rooms clash, charg-
ing at the door.

Luckily, when they brought five starving ferrets in a
wooden box, I had the sense to stand on the teacher's table. I
mean this has happened before, hasn't it, and I gave an
impromptu dance lesson from there. But nature lessons are a
bit of a risk because there's always old reproduction. For 3B
there's only old reproduction. You daren't ask, "Now have
you any questions?" because the questions are of the "What is
Durex, Miss?" "Why don't prostitutes have babies?" or "Do
you use Tampax?" variety. And with my menopausal flush-
ings as well as my normal blushings, I'm afraid those are out.

By the end of the summer term 3B had me reduced to a
sort of whimsy wraith. I moved among them like one of
those Pre-Raphaelite females, ineffectual, meaningless, with
a drawn kind of look about me, like a hen in the moult. I
remember the last lesson; Shanks had just heard that he'd got
a job in an abattoir and spent his time practising to kill in a
corner and glowing with an aura of death, while Robinson
was decorating his books, his school bag, his hands with
swastikas. I asked him why, he said he liked them. Why?
"They're nice and cruel, Miss." And poor Sullivan was still
sucking his thumb and he was going down to the docks next
week. Yes, all right, I know they were tragic and I did worry
about them, but it was a pity for me, too.

It wasn't 3B who were the last straw that term though, but a visiting female instructor from the Ministry, or the Education Department, or some such place. There was a senior boy going in for a drama scholarship and I was helping him with his elocution.

If you've never taught in a school you can have no idea of the problems of finding a room. If you have taught, then you'll know what I mean. There wasn't an empty classroom where I could take this boy; gym was going on in the hall, parents were in the careers room, electricians in the little place under the stairs. Finally, in despair, I took him to the ladies' lavatory – there simply wasn't anywhere else. Actually it's not just as bad as it sounds because there's a cloakroom, with a washbasin and coat hooks first, and the actual lavatory, the pan, the paper and the notion of it, are all in a little separate room beyond, a little roof just big enough to hold the brush and bin and let you turn to reach the paper.

For a reason I've never discovered there's an armchair in the cloakroom and I sat in this, in the umbrage of other people's coats while the boy, Garrett, stood at the door to the lavatory. He was a good-looking boy, with crisp, dark hair that grew low on his brow and an oddly gentle tone to his skin, not girlish, more like that of an old, old woman who is content. His eyes were thickly lashed and a deep, passionate sort of blue and it was obvious that, if you liked chickens, he'd be your dish. I don't personally go for chickens. His voice was good, but he was struggling to hide his Cardiff Market vowels with a nasty la-di-dah copied off Welsh B.B.C. announcers and he also had this unfortunate inability to keep still. He either fidgeted his fingers in an annoying meany way or made wild uncontrolled, uncoordinated gestures.

I nagged about relaxing and the need for repose as I sat there slumped in my chair, but the minute he concentrated on forgetting the nasty vowels he'd begin waving again.

"Garret, will you for heaven's sake keep still, boy?"

"Miss, I keep forgetting, Miss."

"Well, this is hopeless. You're wasting my time. Look, let's try it like this," and up I got and took both his hands and put them behind him, clasped. "Keep your hands there, like that," I said, standing in front of him with my back to the door, voluminous in my academic gown.

"Now, we'll try it again" and, still holding him, I looked up at his face. But his face had gone rigid and red and he was staring at the door like somebody watching the approach of a big black spider. I spun round, guilty as forty thieves, because this cloakroom was really no place to be, and she was standing there, speechless, appalled, affronted in a tweed skirt and twin-set.

Before I could get a word out, she banged the door and left. I looked for her all over that school but I never found her. She thought the worst and who could blame her? I told the Head and he laughed till he died but he told me her name and I said I'd write and explain. But I never did, you know how you don't. She'd gone and I never got down to it and everybody else laughed so I laughed too. But I worried on the quiet and it added to my burdens, all those awful small hours burdens that haunt my nights and that I never act on in my days. If some of my husband's psychiatrist friends analysed me on the basis of the things I neglect to do, I think they'd say I was a would-be suicide. The things I ought to put right, the impressions I ought to correct and don't. It's accidé, I suppose, one of the seven deadly sins.

That last day of term was a pouring summer day, a bedraggled old day, even the City Gardens all frumpish and droopy. Terraced houses mean and shifty-looking, the municipal buildings streaked and dirty like wedding cakes left out in the rain. I travelled home to my suburb in a streaming red bus, everybody in it all cancelled out in macs and rain hats. I felt more cancelled out than most. Isolated in a fawn mac the colour of nothing and a rain hood I couldn't be bothered to take off. A plastic hood that had me jailed in my misery. I didn't even flick a smile at the City Hall as we passed it though I usually salute it out of respect to a friend of mine who claims to have a pile that feels like the dome of the City Hall.

End of term. I should be rejoicing, but that twin-set woman and 3B and their little futures had between them pushed me into a kind of posture of misery, a self-indulgence of gripes which I could any minute now turn into one of my melodramatic despairs. We'd been reading The Prelude in the Sixth and the ecstasy and the magnificence had taken me up, the power and the glory, and now "as high as we have mounted in delight, in our dejection do we sink as low". My soul was full of echoes, undone vasts, rejections; nameless sorrows had me by the throat, my soul felt rough, like a cheese grater, like steel wool. The windscreen wipers in the driver's cabin repeated power and glory – gone – for ever and ever – gone – amen and amen – for ever – gone – amen so be it – gone.

The bus stopped but the wipers went on nagging as I waited to get off, and as I pushed, vitriolic, to the steps I muttered, "To hell with Amen; so be it, my foot. Lady, we receive but what we give, and what we are bloody well determined to grab".

I like our house, it's old and stable and relaxed. I've got some fine old pieces of furniture and the patina on them is soothing and soft, but coming in on that horrid, wet old day I hated the place. It was so continuous, so permanent, smug and self-sufficient. Like a deep-bosomed mum, the kind I'm not, all cottonwool and white tissue paper. I wished I could put a tent up in the garden, to hide in there, an empty green tent with grass on the floor, but it was raining and I'm a bit old for damp gestures. Still wearing my mac and hood I walked about the house hating and then I spat plumb in the middle of my old, perfect oak trestle table and said aloud into the embracing silence, "Oh, bugger off".

I was a bit less bloody-minded by the time my husband, Mike, came home from his evening surgery in his galoshes – I ask you, galoshes and his plastic mac still showing the creases where he'd folded it neat. I was better tempered because I'd been upstairs to sort out my clothes and make a list of what to pack for my holiday. Mike and I were going to Yugoslavia. I love lists. I had some new dresses I'd put off wearing to keep them sort of pristine for the sun. You know how it is, when you're planning and you stroke the lid of your suitcase and click the locks to hear the satisfying noise of them and you remember the feel of the sun and hot sand and it's raining outside. I had everything on my list, from enterovioform and an air freshener – those abroad lavs – to my evening slippers and my squirrel stole for chilly evenings and no bloody mac and rain hat.

Don't get me wrong. I've got a lovely husband, I'm so close to him that I think of him more as an adjunct of me than a separate person, but the sight of him in that mac and those galoshes worked on me like an attack of heartburn. He looked so daft in them. You know the way a plastic collar doesn't cling to the human frame, but stands away from the neck and makes you old and naked-looking, sort of revealed and innocent? The lunatic didn't take off his rain things, he just stood there in the dining-room door, dripping, and said "Look, darling, I've got to tell you at once. Something rather dreadful has happened. Wilson's ulcer has blown up again and I shall have to go to that conference in his place. You know how I hate conferences and in Coventry at that."

"To hell with how you hate Coventry. It's in September, isn't it? What about our holiday?"

"Yes, I know. I'm sorry, lovie, but we'll have to postpone it."

"Postpone nothing. The kids'll be home till September and my mother comes in October. That fortnight was our only chance and you bloody well knew it. Damn Wilson and his ulcer, has there been any plan yet that that hospital of yours hasn't ruined for us? And will you in the name of all that's holy take off those damn galoshes?"

I went and sat in an armchair and sulked and he poured me a glass of sherry, but I ignored it and lit a fag instead, tearing the smoke down like life-blood because he hates me to.

Then, tired and childish, I started to cry. I cried sobbing and pushed him away from me. It wasn't only disappointment, part of it was guilt, because I didn't really have anything to cry about, I wanted to cry dramatic and I was only crying spoilt.

And he was so kind and so apologetic and I knew all the time he was being tolerant and remembering my age and all THAT. Isn't it horrible when people are understanding? How dare they understand? What impertinence, what bloody cheek.

"I will not be understood. Don't do it. Stop it. Stop it."

"Then pull yourself together, Innes, and stop this hysteria." That word again, hysteria, from the Greek for uterus. "Look is there any reason on God's earth why you shouldn't go alone? What's to stop you?"

"What's to stop me? Me, of course," I said, my voice all catarrh and my eyes swimming. "I couldn't go alone, I'd die."

He is nice; he went down on his knees in front of me and put his arms around me; I didn't mind that sort of understanding, he always knew what my body wanted.

"Come now, darling, look you could have a lovely time. You'll meet interesting people. Chaps are always going on their own. Think of all those spinsters."

"But I haven't been alone in a hundred years. You lose the habit. And people are frightened of solitary people. I am myself."

"Rubbish, you often insist on being alone, you know you do."

"Only if I know you are there somewhere and I'm safe from pity. Nobody ever believes a woman is alone from choice and they'll take one look at me and my face and think they understand why I'm alone. And horrible women might come and want to be friends with me and invade me and I'd have no defences."

I wasn't actually crying any more, only sniffling and beginning to realise how terrible I must look with red rimmed eyes, a streaming, naked nose, and my hair in a mess from his stroking it. But I couldn't ask him to stop, not at this stage in the crisis. In fact I was already feeling much better for my weep, you do at my age, but I wasn't telling anybody. But I drank my sherry and allowed myself to be comforted and cosseted and indulged. By the end of the evening my bad temper and disappointment had been elevated and magnified to the proportions of excusable and justifiable menopausal despair and Mike was insisting that I must go on holiday if only on medical grounds.

CHAPTER 2

If I hadn't been in one of my despairings when Mike told me his holiday was postponed, I could have handled the disappointment and been a good wife. Only it hit me when I was down, when I was no good to man or beast, and I took up this bloody-minded, selfish, will-full posture and once I'm in a posture it's like cement. I have to get out of it quick or it sets. I let it set. What's so frightening about keeping a posture is the irrationality, the conscious rejection of your own good sense, you're so stubborn you won't even give yourself a hearing. I didn't want to go on holiday on my own, I knew I'd be lonely and miserable and self-conscious, I knew I'd hate it, but I was possessed – that word is quite right – I was possessed by a wickedness that drove me, goaded me. He'd said I needed to go and I damn well would. I wanted to spite the world and one way to do it was by spending a lot of money we couldn't afford on a holiday I wouldn't enjoy, by asserting the poor rag of my independence, a tattered banner of an old thing that I don't want anyway. I like to be dependent, spoilt and cosseted, I'm very feminine. Only this feeling of cancellation that I'd allowed to catch me was so black, so blotting, I had to kick it, and it was my world, everything I loved, especially those I loved.

Providence sent me plenty of warnings against going. There was the problem of having to share a room with a strange female instead of Mike, for a start. I didn't fancy that one small bit, she might even have dentures in a tumbler. Then Providence warned me again by having the cleaners lose my red suede suit, but I wasn't listening to Providence. Providence was in the dog-house with all the rest of them. I'd planned to travel in this suit because it's a gay and friendly colour and a suede suit is most certainly not middle-aged, is it? It's a good colour for my hair, too, I used to be fair, the colour they call honey and my hairdresser is good at keeping it that way. The only other thing my face has to commend it are my eyes which are a funny hazel green and large. But after that, it's a travesty, honest. I have a little pug nose just like a Pekinese and under that a big wide mouth full of teeth. My mouth is three times as long as the widest part of my nose, I know because I've measured it. Do you know that tame chimpanzee called Judy on Television? Right, you've got it.

As I was saying, for weeks and weeks that red suit could-n't be traced; it was only on the day that I was leaving that it turned up at the cleaners, I suppose the destiny that shapes our ends gave up when it was obvious that I wasn't to be rea-soned with and allowed the suit to be found. I had to change into it on the train from Cardiff to London. I wished it could have been a wet and miserable old day when I left, to give me some kind of excuse for going, but it was a soft, gently warm evening. The train was hot and crowded, dusty and indifferent, and I sat there like a sultana in a yashmak of small bits and pieces of left-over luggage with the cleaners' parcel on top. Only my eyes peeped over them, hard with resolve to do what I didn't want, brittle with my lying hopes.

Half-way to London I went down the corridor to change my clothes. I needn't tell you what that place was like on a crowded train and nowhere to hang anything and gentlemen not lifting the seat, but I came back in my red suit and my best alligator shoes, these were my comforts, shield and buckler against the horrors of my holiday.

I escaped after a while into a jerky train sleep and when I half awoke we were in Swindon and it was dusk. I shuffled to comfort my feet in the alligator shoes – too smart for Wales, too tight for anywhere – but my shufflings were menaced by a low and thunderous growl. My eyes flew open like a trap, sheer terror turned my posturing out of doors, for literally at my feet lay the vast and heaving bulk of the largest boxer dog ever conceived by Satan on some monstrous dam. His teeth were grinning half an inch from my ankle, his hot black tongue was lolloping, pulsing; saliva drooled on my best shoes. He'd sneaked up on me, sleeping, and now bubbles of spit panted onto my feet; the heat he gave off was like lifting the lid of a stove. I dared to move my feet a murmur. He looked up at me sideways, brown eyes in a bath of liquid red, then he sighed, lifted his head, grumbled at the indignities of trains and put his jaw down firmly across both my feet, heavy, hot, positive, announced. He didn't seem to belong to anybody, nobody wanted to claim him and he had me.

It was just about then that I remembered my suitcase. All the luggage from the whole holiday Principality was piled hugger-mugger, by the doors. My clothes, my stole, my air-freshener, my confidence, my holiday was somewhere in that pigs-guts of luggage. Someone was bound to take it by mistake. That's another middle-aged thing, these sudden panics you get, like that you've lost your tickets or gone past your station or you've left a pair of rumpled stockings on a chair in the consulting room and the patient is in there.

Wales is a poor country and everybody seemed to have bought their bags at Marks & Spencer's like me. It all seemed to be alike, all of the same reliable, unassuming, cheap, indistinguishable pretensions, dark green, metal trim, safe locks, identical keys. Someone was bound to take mine.

I didn't think they'd steal it, mind, it would be an honest mistake. Let the English say Taffy was a Welshman, Taffy was a thief; no one would purposely steal my holiday. What if the first book ever to be printed in Welsh contained a version of the Ten Commandments that excluded the Eighth, that was an accident too. But my squirrel stole, my one and only, my slinky, silky stole, my new clothes. Oh no, God forbid. Please God forbid and make this dog move to give me a chance to look for it.

He read my thoughts. There was another low, slow, rumbling, undigested growl. So I sat there; from there to Paddington. What was I doing here without my man? You'd have thought such a symbolic dog would have given me pause. A big black dog, I mean what more could Providence have done? But I was still turning a deaf ear and anyway, I found my luggage.

My aeroplane for Yugoslavia was to leave at some godawful small hour but I went straight from Paddington to the smack in the mouth of London Airport to re-pack my bags with the clothes I'd changed in the train and some of my various bits and pieces of clutter. I wanted to check it in and get it safely off my mind. For hours I had to hang around in that place. It was as hot as an American supermarket and just as indifferent. There were millions of people. I was baked in my red suit and my feet hurt. I had to queue for a drink at the bar and the barmen were nasty and young and superior and I was a solitary woman. I hate young barmen, who do they think they are, anyway? I wanted to spit on mine so I offered him a drink out of the change and he said not on duty, thank you madam, which just shows you.

Then I had to queue for the ladies. It was a long, hot, harassed queue, jigging children and anxious mums with face flannels and tall, arrogant *Vogue* types looking surprised and affronted at students in jeans with hair. One of the *Vogue* types was standing in front of me in the queue and we were packed pretty tight. She had on a very smart cream-coloured coat and skirt in a sort of knobbly stuff – bouclé I think you call it – and she was talking to another woman in a suit of black and brown. I can't tell you how dowdy the cream and the black and brown made my cherry red. Made it obvious and almost sordid in the effort to be bright. Made it provincial and me disenchanted.

In the end it was our turn, the cream suit just before me, and we slipped in and there was a bit of peace. In there I decided to take off my jacket, which was cooking me, but when I looked at my cream silk blouse it was covered with little red lumpy flecks. After the cleaners the surface of the suede was coming off all over like measles. I couldn't possibly appear in that and as I struggled back into the jacket again I heard the *Vogue* voices outside.

"My God, darling, just look at your dress. The back is smothered in red flecks."

"Red flecks? What the hell?"

"Red flecks, I promise you. It's ruined my love, it's ghastly."

"Don't just stand there, do something about it. Find the woman and get a clothes brush."

I snatched my hand away from the lock like a captured thief and cowered behind my door. I remembered the length of the queue, the harassed mothers, but I daren't move. They'd kill me. My suit may have been provincial, but it was distinctive. I bet there wasn't another one in London Airport. They'd have my life and who could blame them?

The performance went on, the lavatory woman's voice, cold, cockney and critical, joined the *Vogue* ones.

I daren't move.

I pulled paper and rustled it, pretending. Then I pulled the chain but I'd put in so much paper it wouldn't go down and the water came up to the rim of the pan and threatened to overflow. Then it gurgled with a rasping sort of cough and most of it went away. The sound of the chain must have cheered somebody up in the queue but I was still too scared to come out. They rattled the door at me – it was probably one of the mothers – but I groaned and in a thin, weak voice I said "Just a minute" and they went away. But still the brushing and the loud voices went on outside. They were so close I could hear the rasp of the brush. They were having a hard time with those flecks, I knew, I'd been trying to pick off a few of my own in a kind of frenzy to destroy the evidence. I was doing my imitation of that chimpanzee I so resemble. She chatters her teeth, clashing them together to indicate disapproval or distress and I've done it so often I found myself, in there, doing it for real, especially when the cockney voice came and rattled the door. "Are you all right in there?" she asked, considerate as a sergeant major.

"Yes, just leave me in peace a minute. It's something I ate."

"There's people waiting," and she threw "madam" at me, like a bad tomato.

"I know, I know. I'm coming."

And then I had to.

They were still working away with the brush, with their backs towards me, but the mirrors were in front of them, they only had to raise their heads. The woman was standing at the door waiting for me, officious, her nostrils dilated, the cloth in her hand. I gave her two separate shillings, in case she thought it was a penny. She looked me over before going in with her cloth, assessing the damage by the size of the tip, but I ran and ran and found peace on a sort of balcony where they have tables and where all the waiters and cleaners are soft, gentle Indians in turbans and I hid there and watched the sparrows that live in the light fixtures and they were my company.

If I'd had anyone but the sparrows with me I wouldn't have been in such a state, so hotly apprehensive, such a Taffytowndilly, scuppered and scared. I was convinced those women were going to Yugoslavia on my plane and they'd be bound to catch me there, I was afraid of their voices and their arrogance, their smartness; I should have realised they weren't charter flight to Yugoslavia types, the very things I was afraid of should have told me, but I couldn't relax, it was like that black dog all over again. Then I heard a plane for

Majorca announced and I watched them go down for it and I could come out again.

I went and got another drink – there was nothing else to do – and then in the final, bitter beginning it was my aeroplane.

Providence gave me a last break at the Immigration Desk, but who was I to recognise the hand of fate? I handed over my passport, but they shook their heads over it and said it wouldn't do, that I couldn't travel on it, that it wasn't mine. I thought we'd all gone mad, that we were in a sort of Kafka situation – the small hours, the harsh official lights, the cold official faces denying my small identity.

"But there's my photograph, for heaven's sake. What's the matter with you, have you gone mad?"

"No, madam, we are none of us insane, but this passport does not belong to you. You cannot travel on it."

"Doesn't belong to me? Of course it belongs to me. Look, there's my photograph I keep telling you."

They looked at me as if they'd like to arrest me and I already felt arrested, there in the middle, holding everything up.

"Come to one side, please," they went on, "and let the other people pass." Humble and alone, I moved out of the queue and a man came to another desk with my passport. "Over here, please," he said, in a voice as cold and closed as a steel filing cabinet.

"Look, madam, this passport belongs to your husband, not to you. If you look here on page 4 you'll find it states specifically that a wife may not travel alone on a joint passport. I'm sorry, but we cannot let you go. We have no assurance that you are using this passport with your husband's consent."

That's the emancipation of women for you, that's the twentieth century.

"I'm sorry, but we cannot take the responsibility for letting you go."

Oh God, I'd come all this way, waited all those hours, endured the dog and the *Vogue* glamour pussies, accepted all that guilt, strung up my resolution, made such a play, and now I had to go back, pathetic. Pathetic, that's the word, the very word that's like a knell for me. I fear pity worse than death, I couldn't face their pity. I'd hide in London and pretend to be in Yugoslavia. What about picture-postcards and suntan? I could get suntan out of a bottle, but the cards? Pretend they'd all got lost in the post? No, I'd never keep it up. It was hopeless. Oh, damn it all to hell.

I didn't move away. Couldn't.

"We could let you go at your own risk, but you might not be allowed into Yugoslavia. That's the problem. They'd probably send you straight back." Cold official faces under cold peaked caps, black uniforms with tarnished gold. "We'll just take your luggage off the plane, if you'll give me your ticket and baggage tag, madam."

All the other passengers were going through and looking at me, watching my misery; perhaps they thought I was an escaping crook or an international agent caught with the blue-prints, but I think they were sorry for me, cherry-suited, whatever I was. I still couldn't bring myself to move away. You'd have thought I'd welcome this final irrevocable excuse, this trump card. Not me, my loins were girded up, my armour was on, the gadfly was feeding on my heart, pricking at my poor menopausal soul, and my pride was killing me. So were my feet.

The immigration man had taken away my ticket and I went on standing alone at his desk, staring at that worthless passport. All the passengers were away now and the place was empty of everything but officialdom.

I couldn't let it go. I threw the passport down and felt the menace in me sprouting and rushing red to my face, "Look," I bawled at the group of idling immigration officers, "don't

just stand around being bureaucratic and fancying your-
selves. There must be something you can do."

One of them came up to me then and he had his cap off
and there was a gentleness and sympathy in his face without
the cap that nearly had me in floods.

"You know, if it was me," he said, "I'd risk it. They want
foreign currency in Yugoslavia and I don't see them turning
yours away. Are you prepared to risk it? If you are, I'll tell
the air line people. You'll still have to pay your fare, whether
they let you in or not – if you think it's worth it."

I said yes, I'd risk it. That fare was a big lump of money,
but do you think I stood there thinking of alternative uses for
it? Not on your Nelly. I signed it away on their official forms
without a thought for kids, carpets, curtains or calamities.
Talk about a bolting horse and bits between the teeth, you'd
think that early morning, I'd never been saddled, mounted,
tamed. But I had, you see, I had, that was the rub. That's why
I bucked.

The other passengers were long since in the aeroplane,
seat belts fastened, cigarettes out, impatient, delayed by the
search for my suitcase that had to be found and taken off and
all the others repacked again. I felt like a leper when eventually I climbed in to join them. They looked at me and specu-
lated.

My aloneness really hit me then. I was clumsy finding a
seat, self-conscious, watched, my shoulder bag of bits and
pieces bumped the seats, my hair-do was collapsing and a
long stray hair was in my mouth. I lifted a hand to brush it
away but my handbag was in that hand already and I hit
myself on the chin with it with everybody looking. I felt like
that small man in a cartoon, my confidence eroded down like
a rotten little milk-tooth in a child's mouth.

I have a look of "effortless superiority" which I can
assume in moments of personal crisis if a little of my confidence remains, but not then, not there. If only I'd had some-

body with me, anybody. Company is such a valid passport, the public evidence that somebody cares about you. Why should I mind what these anonymous faces thought about me, but I did, God, how I did. I felt goose-fleshed by the watching eyes and there wasn't an empty seat till the very end of the plane and then I was able to hide there but I couldn't even light a fag for company.

When the girl came round offering refreshments I found myself ordering a double vodka and lime in a loud and positive, unnatural voice. A double vodka at three o'clock in the morning. Here's a start.

I'd promised the family to keep a sort of diary of my holiday so I thought I'd begin then, all tiddly as I was with vodka. But I had nothing to write on, only the vomit bag tucked sedately into the seat in front of me, so I wrote on that and this is what I wrote –

I begin this chronicle very suitably on a vomit bag. Here I sit like a refugee in a limbo of uncertainty. It's some small hour, which doesn't matter, and I've just finished a double vodka. I'm rather shocked at myself but feel quite justified for I am now in an euphoric haze, feeling restored.

I hope I may be allowed to land. But I must face it, I'm not travelling as a white, fairly Christian, married, respectable woman, husband in tow, in charge. I'm a suspect, perhaps fleeing on my husband's passport without his consent. With an invalid passport and without a visa, I'm off behind the Iron Curtain. Goodbye England, Goodbye Wales. I'm off to Aberdare.

Oh, there's drunk I am. You know, the forties are like creeping alopecia, honest, patches of emptiness that threaten to join.

I wonder who I'll have to share a room with if I am allowed to land. She may be godawful but we can go our separate ways, surely. I'm being nasty and anti-social about that woman, but honestly, I can't be blamed, not really. If people only realised what it means to share a bedroom with older sisters for all your formative years, they'd sympathise. People say large families are a good thing, they don't begin to appreciate that the littlest ones suffer real maternal deprivation, walled away by big sisters. They were so pretty and I was so small, such a duckling. I must have been an awful pest, so little, so needing care, so demanding, such a cry baby. I was a bore to them and how it hurt to be a bore, they had an alliance, but I was too young. They kept me in order with dollops of love but mostly with terror. There was the theory they held that the devil came in the night to count your teeth if you'd been wicked in the day, especially if you'd disobeyed your sisters. Why count your teeth?

Not such a terrible punishment. But I can still feel the horror of a scaly beast with a tail and long pointed ears who would sit on your chest and open your mouth and slowly count your teeth. It is horrible, isn't it? It's sexy, now I come to think of it, and why have I never really thought about it like that before? And what in the name of all that's holy has this to do with a middle-aged woman who may or may not be about to begin a lovely holiday abroad with sunshine and wine and waiters. I must be mad. Is there more here than a double vodka?

I'll change the subject. There's not much room left on this bag. I could open it out, I suppose and write on the inside. No, that's waterproof, of course. I must say some of the other passengers look much more suspect than I do. There's a restless one in a grey-striped seer-sucker jacket who keeps walking about, showing off. He's a baddie for sure. And there's one who keeps picking his nose, avid. And what a nose. It's the shortest, broadest, nothing of a nose, worse than mine. There's a gorgeous Indian beside him with a strong, purposeful, hooked nose, and sculptured lips. His eyes are closed, superior. Somebody, I can't see him, is reading tomorrow's *News of the World*. I can see the headlines.

Secret vices, 100 cigarettes a day. Branded for a Weddingday Scandal. Liquid Dynamite – Violence in a Pool.

FOR YOUR CONVENIENCE. In case of sickness call stewardess for disposal.

I didn't write that, it was on the bag already and had a kind of halting, prohibitive effect. I went to sleep.

CHAPTER 3

They let me into Yugoslavia without as much as a first
thought, leave alone a second one, and as I climbed into the
bus that would take me to my hotel I was feeling pleased no
end with myself. It wasn't till the bus moved out and into the
country that I began to feel on holiday, to feel abroad. Worry
is such a bore, so inhibiting, doesn't let you dream or appreciate, it's like being blind or very poor. I wasn't feeling
lonely now, too full of myself, too bucked. Loneliness is a
hell of an unpredictable thing.

There was a grey light in the sky already and I could see
the unmistakable arthritic silhouettes of olive trees, the stark
fingers of cypresses and the hideously exotic prickly pears.
Dawn was pushing blue grey through the olive groves and
when the bus stopped beside somebody else's hotel, the flat,
thick leaves of a fig tree slapped against my window, bright
apple green in the hotel lights. The bus went on, passed a
harbour full of ships, passed a sheet of sea the colour of old
cannons with nobody in it but the fishes; the silent suburbs
closed around us, shuttered and shut, big white concrete cubes
of hotels and the skeletons of more and more new ones.

In the end it was my hotel and now nearly full dawn. I was
the last one in the bus and I got out and the driver came to
collect my luggage from a sort of cavern under the bus. But
the cavern was empty. Nothing. No suitcase. We looked at
each other. He shrugged his shoulders. The driver spoke only
Serbo-Croat, but Coffer is universal. "Coffer," I said.
"Coffer, drug?"

But he shook his head and shrugged again, a bewildered,
sympathetic shrug and said "Agency Turistico. Telephono."
So I shrugged too – what else could I do, in the dawn in
Yugoslavia with sixteen words of Serbo-Croat at my

command? Tourist Agencies were said to be efficient. It would come tomorrow, yes, it would come tomorrow, but, Watchman, what of the night? Well, there wasn't much night left. Don't fuss.

The driver came up to the hotel with me and spoke to the night porter, explaining, I imagine, about the lost luggage. I didn't exactly take to the night porter. He was tall, thin, grey-faced (fair enough in a night porter, no doubt), black, black-haired, and he had these eyes. He stooped because of his height and bogus humility and held his head on one side so his eyes looked sideways at you and were the most kytodiascopic I've ever encountered. (In case you don't care for etymology, kytodiascopic is one of Mike's words, from Kyto, Greek, a shirt, i.e., see through your shirt.) I said I encountered his eyes, but 'encountered' there is ill used, because you never did, in fact, encounter the eyes, they slid, all over and around and about, exploratory, like Donne, Oh, my America, my Newfoundland. He was only about twenty-four, I think, and I now believe he must have been troubled with an Oedipus complex, it's not uncommon in Yugoslavia, as I was to discover. On the other hand, he may simply have been a realist and turned to the older woman out of despair over making a young one, just a case of playing in his own league. I ought to have been a bit sympathetic because I too knew about playing in the right league, but, after all, there are leagues and leagues and not even I am relegated to the fourth division yet.

He took me up to my room on the first floor and the lift was small and tight, but not as tight as he made it out to be and all in silence, mark you, for I was far too tired and put off to try out any of my sixteen words. He rested one elongated hand on the side of the lift so that incidentally, as it were, it was suspended over my shoulders and he had a humble, eager dog's smile and all the time the eyes were exploring, assessing. I felt positively affronted. I have to use that nineteenth century word, he made me feel nineteenth century, sort of rigid.

He put his finger to his lips when we stopped at the door of what I trusted was to be my room and said "Bella donna". Was he calling me bella donna? If he was, it was the quickest seduction attempt and biggest lie on record. But the bit of Italian was handy, I hate silence, and I could say "Subito, subito, per favore", and he opened the door and there indeed was the bella donna, asleep in one of the two beds, with the light on and a book slack in her hand.

The porter was looking at her, agog, like a fourteen-year-old reading a dirty book, and at once I was for her, all the way.

"Grazie," I said to him and firmly shut the door on his greed, on the horrible incongruity of it. I had to protect her, even before she knew I was there I had a role, I had a relationship with her, whatever she would feel about me, and the thought of him with a pass-key gave me the creeps. The thought of him just standing there looking was worse than rape.

In my shoulder bag I had, thank God, my washing things and cosmetics and a pair of sandals I'd bought on the way to the train. I put my toothbrush into the same glass as hers and it felt companionable. The sight of a tin of air freshener standing beside the glass led me to hope I'd found a friend. There were no dentures. I had no nightie, of course, so I thought I'd go to bed in my petticoat but there again the bloody old suede had come off all over and I didn't dare wear it to bed because of the sheets. There was nothing for it but my nakedture. As I threw back the clothes, starkers, she opened one blue eye and said "Hullo. Thank God you're not modest, anyway, that solves one problem. They charge 3/6 for a bath."

"Hi," I said, "see you in the morning," and we slept and then it was really morning and I was half awake and I heard a voice.

"Will you tell me something. Why the hell are you naked?"

"The bastards have lost my luggage," I said, remembering, "Sorry to shock you."

"I'm not shocked. No, we're going to share this room for a fortnight and I refuse to pay 3/6 for a bath. There's going to be a deal of nakedness about the premises." She was sitting up in her bed in a pale blue nightie with lace insertions. Her shoulders were broad and powerful and her head seemed to ride on them like a buoy. A neat head, the bright auburn hair swept up in a lavish bun and the back of her neck trim and delicate. Her face was almost classically beautiful but redeemed by a silly little twist in the middle of her nose. She was assessing me with sharp blue eyes as I lay there, flat, fagged. "We'll have to get on, you know."

"Yes, we'd better, hadn't we? I'll tell you the worst, quick, so we can give up the pretences. I'm Welsh, I drink, I smoke, I vote Labour, I'm menopausal and liable to depressions, I'm married, I've got three grown up kids, two boys and a girl. My husband is a doctor in Cardiff, but we've got an overdraft. I teach part-time and I'm bad-tempered in general but the thing that gets me fighting mad is racialism."

"Yes, I saw you were married. Me too, but I've got six kids, not grown up. That's why I came, had to get away. There they are, look, all my kids. I've just been saying good morning to their pictures."

I took the photograph and held it up over my face. "Nice," I said, "that your husband?"

"I'm a Roman Catholic."

"Oh, yes. You don't curse like a Roman Catholic. Why do you say it like a confession of guilt?"

"Where I come from it is a confession of guilt. Were you ever in Northern Ireland?"

"Oh, of course, that's your accent. I couldn't place it. No, I've never been. Do you come from Belfast?"

"No. Ballyduggan. My man's a Crown Solicitor."

"I wondered about the six kids. You a nationalist?"

"No, politics drive me nuts."

"But you don't really have politics over there, do you? I got the impression you only had God."

"Not too much of him, either. What's this they call you?"

"Gibson. Innes Gibson. What's yours?"

"Joan. Joan Maguire. Jesus, where's the breakfast?"

"I forgot to order it. Did you?"

"How in the name of God could I order it? I can't say a bloody word to them. I only found out about the bath from a wee Scotch body last night. I know money's only money but I ordered a room with bath and here, they're asking 3/6 a time. I won't be conned, sure I won't. Ring yon bell beside you and see what happens."

"And get that Quasimodo, that night porter up here with me in my nothings? Not a bloody hope."

"Here, put on my dressing gown and see what you can do," so I did that and a young chamber-maid came and I said "Dobor dan" and then abandoned Yugoslav and said "Café, per favore."

"No," Joan said, from her bed, "tell her I want tea, with lemon, please."

"Te con limone per Signora."

"Si, signora."

"Chvalar" I said, reverting, as the girl went out.

"Whatever was that last word you said?"

"Chvalar. It's thanks in Serbo-Croat. You ought to learn it, it's handy."

"Chvalar – Oh, to hell, you say it for both of us. And I'll tell you something else. I can't cope with this currency. Sure it's no holiday if you've got to count the ruddy cash and do sums. Will you do the paying and we'll settle up afterwards? I was never abroad alone before, were you?"

"No. Were you scared to come?" I asked, getting back into bed.

"No time to be scared. I had to run or go mad. Six kids, Jesus, Mary and Joseph! Why are you on your own, anyway?"

"I'm not sure. Well yes, I'm alone because my husband had to go to a conference at the last minute, but I had to run too, nothing to run from, but partly for spite and partly a sort of awful panic, a panic to grab, with my being in the change. I get this feeling of losing everything, I'm even out of touch with myself, you know? And scared rotten, honestly."

"Sure, you're daft, woman dear. What's wrong with you at all?"

"Well, like I said, I don't quite know and I'm so out of touch with myself I don't even know whether I'm inventing half my symptoms and enjoying the drama of the menopause or not. But I think this sort of sense of loss I have is genuine. It's a kind of empty fear, like waking up suddenly and finding you've been asleep with the door open."

Joan was registering the most old-fashioned look of bright-blue-eyed scepticism and I hurried on to try and make myself sound a bit more reasonable. "Well, I'll tell you, it's like living in a nasty dream where you're looking everywhere for something, and you're heavy and clumsy and the loss is killing you and you don't know from nothing what you've lost. Like that. It's only the change. It'll go. But listen, about the currency and that, I never count my change, never look, just take what they give me."

"Good, me too. That's great. But don't let's have too much of that sense of loss crap. It'll get on my nerves and we've got to try and get on."

The breakfast tray came, the thick cups, the tinny cutlery, that object for squeezing the lemon slice, the lovely butter, the rolls and apricot jam masquerading as marmalade, It began to feel lovely, to feel abroad.

"I'll have to go down to collect my bag, I suppose. It's bound to be here by now. Shall I give them a break and go down like this?"

"Listen, will you not ring that bell again and ask the wee girl?"

"I can't say all that in Italian. I'm out of practice and I've quite forgotten the word for lost. I don't think she knows much Italian anyway, probably as much as I know in Serbo-Croat, sixteen words. I'll have to put on that suit again and in this heat. Just look at the sun on that balcony. I'm going to stand in it. I must."

I pulled on yesterday's pants and brassiere and, coffee cup in hand, I threw aside the lace curtains, barged open the mosquito nets and stepped out to the sun, hoping for a view of cypresses and the sun-bright Adriatic and found myself almost nose to nose with a builder's labourer working on a new bit of the hotel only yards away from me. He took off his straw hat and made me a low bow while I retreated, tangled in curtains and spilling cooling coffee down my front.

Joan was killing herself in bed, "Oh God take care of us. Did you see the look of him, and him in his straw hat? God forgive me for laughing" and she went off again into peals.

"Listen," I said, trying to mop coffee off my bra and out of my navel, "I promise you I'd die if I put on a suede suit this morning. The heat out there would blister you, shouldn't be surprised if I've got blisters on my feet already. Could I borrow something of yours just to go down and collect my things? I'd sweat blood in suede, honest."

"Of course you can. I'm so bloody tall though that's the problem, and big with it. Let's have a look. If you had a shift, straight, the fit wouldn't matter. It's the length worries me." She swung out of bed and I saw what she meant about being bloody tall. She could give me a good four inches, I saw again what Quasimodo had meant by the "bella donna". She must have been five foot ten and the six kids had left few traces on her figure. But her feet were a shock, for her toes were hunched together hideously and each one glistened hard with corns. Unlike the let-down of her nose, I didn't find the feet endearing. I hate ugly feet, they'll put me off as easily as dentures.

"Don't look at my feet. I can feel you looking."

"Sorry. I've got a thing about feet."

"Me too, but I was brought up poor and my mother crushed my feet in other people's shoes. Now let's have a look." She opened the wardrobe door and it was full of clothes, enough for weeks and weeks.

"Staying long?" I asked.

"Oh to hell, I like them all, couldn't bring myself to leave them behind. What about this? Try it."

It was a tea-coloured linen shift, a gorgeous dress, far too good to lend, but I slipped it over my head and it came down well below my knees in these days of mini-skirts. I looked like Orphan Annie, slack, long, neglected.

"It was Christmas day at the Workhouse, but I can go as far as the reception desk in it, sure you don't mind? Don't laugh now, or I won't dare."

"It's not so bad, honestly it's not. And sure it's only for a few minutes. Away now and see if your case is there."

When I'd thought about this holiday at home in Cardiff and about my being alone on it, I'd imagined myself coping in my own clothes, getting confidence from their fit, their trimness on the still good old figure, from the smart newness of them, the way they sort of underline the eccentricity of my face, like a macabre, witty remark. I go for downward stripes and odd colours, like waving the standard when all but he had fled. Orphan Annie had had no place even in my nightmares.

There was no suitcase. I was advised to call in person at the Tourist Agency.

But I couldn't face the world six inches below the knee and as Joan got washed and dressed I sewed a hem up on the dress. I made it shorter, certainly, but the white cotton stitches showed up on the tea-coloured fabric and the hem, unpressed, stuck out, obvious as a coloured patch on a pair of trousers. There was a wide embroidered border around the edge of the skirt and my sewing cut it in half and made it so small as to be simply stupid. I looked like an old deprived child, but it was necessary to laugh, and I did that.

It was a long, hot tram ride from our hotel to the old city. The trams were simply rows of benches of the same yellow hardness as the fumed oak of chapel seats, with a platform at either end and a flat wooden roof and no sides. There were the usual notices about, probably warnings against spitting and requests for the right change, painted on dark blue enamelled plaques, very abroad. The tram was as full as a nut, with people hanging on, like those trains you see in films about India. And there was one abroad thing on that tram that I always hate, the way the girls don't shave and have these big black tufts in their armpits. I hate it. It's so suggestive, if you know what I mean, so animal, so reminiscent.

In our hot and intimate tram we passed by olive trees, grey, twisted, skeletal, like thin old men; the vineyards were blue-green, like cabbage fields and beside the vines grew a sudden fig-tree, bright bright green, and then the unexpected, incredible, quick small flames of ripening pomegranates. The terraced mountains threatened to crowd the tramway into the sea. They shouldered up, fold behind fold into the bright heat and the houses and hotels crouched, terra-cotta roofed, on their reluctant fringes. The houses clung to each other, grasping at the last foothold, seemed piled on top of each other, clinging, climbing, joined by arches, tunnels, colonnades, as elegant as antiquity and submissive as peasants, bowed and shaped by the glaring force of the mountains, the fierce sun and the sea. And then a new hotel, white concrete, hideous, brash, incongruous as, well, as a polar bear.

The city itself was built on an out-thrust of land, like a kick of mountain into the sea. No tramcars nor any vehicles,

no hotels nor new houses were admitted in the antiquity of
the city. From above we could see the Roman, square, solid-
ity of its walls; three challenging the everlasting Adriatic and
the fourth four-square against the menace of the crouching
mountains. We looked down on a jumble of weathered
apricot roofs, on churches and towers sharply white, the
green of the cathedral's dome and the eternity of the grey
walls and parapets. But first I had to find my clothes.

The Tourist Agency was near the drawbridge before the
great city gates and I went in there while Joan stood looking
into shop windows thinking of presents for her kids. I found
no luggage, but I did find Franko. He worked in the Agency
and spoke English and was desolated to discover that my
suitcase was lost. I had to account for my appearance as fast
as I could; without Joan and the blanketing crush in the tram,
I felt all my resolution melting and I gabbled that this dress
was my friend's, that I had nothing. Franko took my hand
and said "Madam, I am desolate. This dress is not good for
you, I know. You do not find yourself. This dress, it is like, I
do not know the word, but such a thing you put – so – over a
candle to put out the light. So – pouf – finish."

What could I do but love him? How did he know so
much? He was only a young man, perhaps thirty, but so
accomplished. Until he spoke to me had had just been a man
in an office that I was prepared to tear strips off, but then I
looked at him properly. He was a sad man, with large, brown,
tragic eyes, his whole face Byzantine, like a crucifixion,
gaunt, a man of sorrows. Such a face must have been a
tremendous advantage in his job, for he dealt with com-
plaints and who could complain in the face of his agony?
Probably why he got the job.

Because he had this crucifixion role he rarely smiled and
this was a very good thing, for most of his teeth were stopped
with aluminium, or whatever it is they use abroad.
Aluminium teeth don't match a Byzantine look and when he

did smile, to reassure me, it was terrible, like Woolworth jewellery on an Italian Madonna.

I'm so aware of teeth. There was that poet in a Peter de Vries novel who hanged himself rather than face life with a mouthful of false ones, I'm like him, I too can tell a bridge-work at ten yards. Teeth are the most middle-aged of all, worse than necks. I watch my friends' teeth like a fox watching chickens and when I see a new smile or somebody off fig rolls and raspberry jam I get a lowness of the spirit from the threat that's as possessive as constipation, dominating as hiccups. There's another of my friends, I dislike her on almost every count but one – she feels like me about teeth. You know when you have a baby, they take away your false teeth for the anaesthetic. This friend of mine had a few towards the front and when she came out of the anaesthetic and was all stitched up and tidied, the first thing she asked was: "Where are my teeth?" not Where's my baby or How's my baby. I know how she felt. That's why she's my friend.

Franko promised to send a telegram at once to London and to search every inch of the local airport and then I left him in sorrowful expectation of the next complaint.

Out in the sun again Joan was standing waiting for me; there was a ring of men around her, at a distance that was fit. You could feel the awed hush of them, the appreciation and respect for this gorgeous capitalista. The man who sold ice-cream from a cart was there, the man selling lottery tickets, the tram conductor, the striped-jerseyed fishermen, a waiter or two, a handful of tourists. I think she was unaware of them, I'm not sure, but anyway, I came up and broke the spell – me the guardian witch.

"No bag?"

"No, but there's a nice man there who's promised to move heaven and earth."

"Will you, for heaven's sake, tell me the price of these things. That wee dress would just suit my Bridget."

"Cross off two noughts and divide by three and you've more or less got it in pounds."

"Pounds? You're kidding."

"No, a 100 is about six bob you see."

"I'm not spending this holiday effing well crossing off two noughts and dividing by three. Can I buy any presents at all?"

"Wait till the end and see what we've got left. Let's go and look at the old City, shall we?"

It was like Venice; the same Renaissance, Romeo and Juliet balconied houses, the white marble streets bright as water in the sun, royal blue awnings, churches, campanile, people, colours. On the fretted stone balconies bright flowers, uncompromising Mediterranean coloured, grew in old tins with the sun-beaten labels still on them, announcing lard and tomatoes, olive oil and tinned beef.

The first building beyond the gate was a church for pilgrims, rose-windowed, simple, ivory coloured, like Bathstone and we turned in there. The church was neglected, hardly tended, its few pictures warped, its floor pitted, damp making maps on the walls and a fist-full of wild flowers in a jam jar on the desolate altar. She genuflected and knelt to pray and I knelt too. You can say thank you even from the fortress of unbelief and it did no harm to whisper a word about my luggage.

The streets were full of people, most of the tourists looking faintly indecent beside the black-clothed peasant women, the busy nuns, the farmers at ease in regional dress and the tall market women in full length, full-skirted costume, embroidered aprons and stiff caps like white birds poised. But far outnumbering them, the fat tourist men in shorts, sleeveless dresses on flabby, red arms, bellies let go under shift dresses and all those ugly feet in open sandals. Horrible. I do wish people had a proper awareness of feet – they're so unashamed. Give me a hairy mole any day before a glossy corn or vein-knotted arches.

We wandered around the small, strange, intimate city, saw one crowded, ostentatious rococo church, nuns and priests abounding, but what price grace? We talked about husbands, children, sea, in-laws, money, clothes. Not yet quite at ease together, feeling the way, assessing, watchful for the boundaries, the personal fortifications.

We saw a nice-looking café and drank slivovitz under an umbrella and the drink was easy and smoothed our paths together, even if it did taste somewhat of French polish. From where we sat at our drinks we saw a notice announcing an exhibition of icons in a dark, cool-looking corner of the city and we went in there. We walked along a sheltered pathway with flowers and shrubs and elegant bits of ancient Rome, broken pillars, heads, tombstones, torsos, milestones. The path ended in a dark cavern, perhaps the dungeons under the city walls. It was a dark, dark place after the sun, and lit only by the concentrations directed at each picture, the rest all black. The icons were golden and imperious, Christ crucified, still in majesty, *pieta* still triumphant. The eyes in them holding you, assessing you and throwing you out; the rejection of the blue madonnas, the arrogance of the saints was blistering, humbling, judicial. What right had you even to question? Yours was to accept, to genuflect, to bow to their cold faith, their wills, their assurance.

There was an old guide who took your money and showed you the icons. Captured and dazed with a new humility I wandered away from Joan, left her talking to some other tourists, from Leeds. She was sociable and easy with people, unlike me, and she liked to chat and pass the time of day.

I went on alone to the furthest cell of the exhibition, uplifted, humbled, awed. The guide followed me and I tried to make halting conversation with him in my shattered Italian and my sixteen words. Perhaps I said something wrong; I may have, unaware, indicated an invitation – I don't know, but I suppose I must give him the benefit of the doubt at least.

He was grinning at me with his aluminium teeth, all three of them, they were all he had and his eyes were a bright lasciv-ious brown in that old, strong face. A kind of warning chill passed through me, there in that macabre, half-lit place, and I turned my back on him as though to look again at one of the Christs. From behind, a strong brown hand cupped my breast while the other hand held me, fingers like pincers, by the chin and turned my head around.

"Cinque minuti," he whispered, his voice harsh, driven. "Cinque minuti. Upstairs. I make good. I haff big. Come."

The shock of it. I mean, three teeth and old, and there under the icons, like in church or on the gravestones. He was much stronger than me and he'd taken his hand away from my breast to pinion my arms. He kept hissing "Cinque minuti" and I couldn't call out properly with that grip on my jaw. All I could do was kick him, but there were no backs to my sandals. Joan heard my half-strangled yelps at last and came walking into this last small enclave and called and he let me go and went away muttering.

Cinque minuti – five minutes – I think that was the crown-ing insult, worse than the three teeth – that one was worth, could be dispensed with in five minutes and finish. My first pass on my holiday – three teeth. That'll learn you, I told myself, you're asking for it, going abroad alone. It's the heat I suppose. He probably thought he was doing me a kindness, looking the way I did in that dress and my age and every-thing. Trying to make conversation is the real danger, I suppose they feel it would be a comfort just to stop our mouths with kisses. *Ych y fi*, with three teeth and dribbles as well, no doubt.

We'd had icons for that day. After lunch we went to the beach. Joan had two bathing costumes and insisted on my wearing her better one, which just shows you. Neither of us was a swimmer so we found a nice shallow pool where we wallowed and sat and sunbathed and read. My books were in my suitcase and all I'd been able to pick up in English in the city was Trollope's *Prime Minister* which is at least long, it would last me, but it's hardly exciting reading. Not what I'd call gripping. But we lay and cooked and read vaguely and watched the baby crabs that thronged on the rocks beside our pool and dozens of them joined us in the water. I was intrigued by them, they were so small and babyish and cheeky and not in the least creepy-crawly.

Then Joan said, "If you saw a spider the size of that baby crab they'd look just the same, wouldn't they now? God, think if all those were spiders, hiving about on the rocks. Look, the rock's moving with crabs."

We didn't fancy the pool much after that and got out and sat tortured on some hard rocks well above the water line. Thinking of spiders and the beach reminded me to pull my bathing costume neat around my crotch and I'll tell you why. It was a day trip we were on, to the sands, and my mother's friend was in a bathing costume that hadn't been over-generously cut. I can remember still the sight of a few escaping pubic hairs, dark against her white skin. I was quite convinced that they were spiders' legs and that she kept spiders in there. The adult world was so strange to me, I could believe anything about it. I was terrified of her after that, wouldn't go near her, but I never told, never said why. If I'd been a small boy it might well have put me off girls for ever and ever, you'd never dare, in case there was the spider in there, lurking, ready to nip you, nip your precious ornament. So I'm always very careful about that, myself.

Suddenly it was cooler, the sun going down, time for sundowners, time to get pansied up. Perhaps my bag would have arrived. I thought about what I'd wear. Cinderella.

We went down together to the dining room. Two drinks at the bar had fortified me to face it, but it was impossible not to feel the looks on me. She was so spectacular, so lovely, she caught the eyes and then of course they strayed to me, me in that slack dress that hung on me as though from a coat-hanger. I looked lost, stolen or strayed. But I was committed not to show I cared much. This was our holiday.

We'd had a table to ourselves at lunch time but now there were a man and woman there before us. As we came up the man stood and bowed and waited for us to sit. A tall craggy sort of fair man with a dark, pretty little woman with bright amused eyes, both younger than I. You could tell from his manners that he was bound to be German. What German did I remember? Damn all for a moment. Wait. "Guten Abend" – hell, that's good day not good evening. Who cares?

"Ah", he said, pleased, "Sie sprechen deutsch?"

"Nein, nein.. sprechen sie englisch?"

"Nein."

"Italienisch?"

"Nein, ach leider nein."

"Franzosisch?" I threw in, despairing.

"Unglucklich, nein." His little wife merely shook her head.

God! Now what? Thank you is "danke" anyway, please is "bitte". In the name of God, I can't remember anything else. She's looking at this dress, fair play, who wouldn't? Baggage is "coffer" anyway. "Meine coffer ist–" God what's lost, delayed? They're looking at me, expectant, Oh where's that damn waiter?

"Ah, Baldo, per favore–" The waiter, Baldo, spoke both Italian and German after a fashion and he explained about the coffer. The little dark woman shook her head and put up her hands in horrified sympathy and I said with a feeble flicker of an apologetic smile, "Ist nicht gut."

"Das ist wirklich schade im Urlaub", he said, giving it all that deep thickness that's like rich food and Dutch stoves.

They didn't like to talk to each other in German and Joan and I felt the same awful constraint. You couldn't not at the same small table, tight like that.

Our bottle of wine came, not exactly vintage claret, but red, at least, and pleasant enough. We'd had it at lunch and it had helped things, for at one level we were still wary strangers.

Joan gestured to the bottle and I said "Wein?" I knew that much at least.

"Danke sehr," he said, tasting it.

"Ist gut?" me.

"Es ist Yugoslawisch," with a shrug. Damn them; because Yugoslav therefore mediocre, by definition. Never mind, let it go. We like it anyway.

I wished I could say I feel like Orphan Annie in this dress, make some sort of joke. Orphanage is Kinderheim. I remember seeing that on a grim wall in the Black Forest, next door to the hospital, Krankenhaus. What good are those words to me? I can't risk Kinderheim, I'll be saying I come from an orphanage and they'll think I'm a real orphan and the looks will deepen. Will you tell me why I'm carrying the burden of this so-called conversation? And why in the name of God is it only me who seems all the time self-conscious? Why not leave it to them for a bit.

Prolonged silence.

I can hear myself eat. Everybody must hear me swallow. My throat's gone constricted with quiet.

I point to the flowers on the table, bouncy, fluffy old mauve and purple asters, horrible, and pink dahlias, worse, like cold flesh. Never mind.

"Schon, nicht wahr?" I say.

"Sehr schon."

Finish.

Oh go to hell, Orphan Annie's bowing out. Yugoslav puddings are always meaningless anyway. We finish the wine, say Gute Nacht and we beat it.

CHAPTER 4

I'd spilt slivovitz down the tea-coloured dress and the dust had clung to the sticky of it in little grey beads. I couldn't wear it again, so we asked the chambermaid to wash it and press up the hem and then the only thing I could conceivably wear from Joan's wardrobe was a black linen button-through sleeveless dress she'd worn early in her last pregnancy. It didn't even fit where it touched, in fact it didn't touch me anywhere except on the shoulders; it was like wearing a box, a long box, just shorter than a coffin.

I decided to live up to it. I tied a black chiffon scarf around my head, put on neither lipstick nor mascara, took off my engagement ring and passed myself off as a peasant. Given an aluminium tooth, you'd never have known the difference. I bowed my head a bit and slumped and practised humility in the bedroom. It was going to be great, complete anonymity. I'd have to run through the hotel but after that it promised to be child's play.

I sat beside Joan on the tram, as though by accident. We'd agreed to cry dumb and not draw any attention to me. People were staring at her, as usual, but she'd acquired this trick of looking unapproachable, like a duchess; not an English horse-faced duchess, but more a Viennese waltz sort of duchess. Nobody noticed me beside her. I sat, looking down at my hands in my lap. They wouldn't do at all, soft and tended as they were. I clenched my fists and was ashamed and thought of Renoir, "all hands are beautiful, as long as they are work-worn". I tucked my pretty feet under the seat, they weren't peasants' feet either, and I suddenly felt ashamed of myself. How dared I be so presumptuous? I'd none of the virtues of a good peasant; flipperty-gibbet, eman-cipated, foolish, depressed, educated, spoilt and I'd had the

40

bloody nerve to pretend I was a peasant. As Joan had said, I needed my bottom warming, so I did. I felt a flush beginning to overwhelm me. It started somewhere in the region of my loins and then tore up to my breasts, my neck, my face and a red fog in my brain. Then the sweat came, around my breasts, between my legs, along my nose and upper lip and pricking my eyes.

An old lady sitting beside me must have noticed and remembered and she put her hand on my arm and spoke to me. I had no idea what she said; I'd already cried dumb and now I had to cry deaf as well. I nodded and smiled and, pointing to my ear, waved my hands in negation and she was filled with compassion for me – deaf and dumb as well! Talk about a tangled web we weave. She handed me a few sprigs of a wild herb she had collected. I don't know what it was, green and feathery and spicy, and I held it in my hand and it was lovely and I felt like the biggest bitch, I just can't tell you.

I could feel the seat heaving as Joan tried to control her mounting giggles and at the next stop I nudged her to get off the tram. I mouthed "Dovegnia" to my elderly friend and went shambling down the steps. Joan was now laughing till her tears were tripping her and, fraud that I am, I laughed as well. I'm a fraud even to myself, because by now I'd forgotten my earlier shame and started to play the peasant again, walking flat and a bit stooped, with my arms held long.

We'd come off the tram at the hospital stop and we passed patients sitting out in the sun in striped pyjamas that had been washed but not ironed; the crumpled, untidy, functional look of those unironed pyjamas would break your heart.

We passed the queue for Casualty, middle-aged women, like me, in black, like me, patient, calm, composed, waiting. Young men with blood-stained bandages and blood on their shirts, old men with sticks, silent children, babies and one man who leaned on his crutches like a soldier resting on his rifle on a war memorial. He was dressed in the remains of bits of army uniform. A forage cap on his head, battle-dress blouse and cavalry breeches with all the buttons undone and one bare foot pushed into a ragged espadrille. The other leg was cased in a battered plaster cast, the dirty toes and blackened nails exposed. His clothes, his fine, prophetic face, seemed to demand a monumental pose and he leaned there like a memorial to resistance, as defeated as a refugee.

Suddenly a taxi charged up the quiet, sunlit street, screaming its urgency, and we stopped and watched. You couldn't have passed on, regardless. Our stopping had nothing to do with vulgar curiosity, we were alerted like wild animals, the two of us and everyone in the queue. You had to wait, life was suspended. They carried a man out of the taxi, a man of about fifty whose face was the colour of dough you've given a child to play with, a sort of grey that isn't a colour at all. The white bristles on his face were stark against that grey, his eyes open, showing only the whites and he was dressed for his holiday, gaudy shirt and dark blue shorts when the blankets fell away from him. The noises he made were continuous, neither screams nor groans, nor anything you could label, nothing human. The sounds seemed to come from his chest and sometimes were like a cow that lows for its calf or a bull bellowing, thirsting for the light, but higher in pitch than that, more asthmatic. And they never changed, never faltered. They carried him in and he was anonymous and we stood there and wanted to cry out. The queue broke up and clustered around the gates, the women cried and talked together. They crossed themselves and beat their breasts and for the first time I knew what the phrase meant, I found myself doing the same.

We could still hear the noises inside. Some of the women grasped the iron railings of the gates and bent their heads and prayed. We heard the jumbled Latin and Joan, my duchess, bowed her head and joined in their prayers, their incantations, if you must. I felt bereft. She, who knew no foreign languages, who relied on me even for please and goodbye, was with them, was truly communicating, had the lingua franca, capitalista in communist Yugoslavia.

I looked at the man with the plaster cast; he was leaning on his crutch, listening to the noises, assessing them, as a soldier might, accustomed to wounds and screamings.

"Is very bad" he said to me in halting English, so much for my peasant disguise – "You have one English cigarette, please? For the noise, it is bad."

"Yes, of course." I passed my pack among the men and they were grateful. So, I too made my communication. But with cigarettes. I would have preferred the prayers.

The noises from inside stopped, dead. The women lifted their heads, listened, hands went up in the sign of the cross and they moved away from the gates and reformed their orderly, disciplined queue. The tension died and slowly we moved away, shivering under the noon-day sun. Franko at the Tourist Agency had naught for my comfort. Today they search in Beograd.

We couldn't go looking at things after the hospital. We'd been too close to crucifixion to enjoy the peace of churches, the ordered calm, the beauty and serenity of salvation. We had to find a drink, quickly, put up a barrier, fast.

Duchess and peasant, we sat at a table together. "That ought to cure you of some of the bloody nonsense you talk. God rest his soul. D'you think he's dead?"

"God knows." I made patterns in the sticky slivovitz spilt on the table. "I feel so bloody small, you know? And Mike, he has it all the time."

"Well, for Christ's sake don't let's have a session on that one now. All right, you're small, unworthy. You've lost something and you don't know what the hell it is, but we've emptied our glasses and we need another one. Away and order them, like a good peasant and will you for my sake please stop thinking?"

When I came back with our new drinks Joan was talking away to two people at the next table. She had a gift for easy, quick, friendly relationships, in spite of the duchess look. These people were Scottish and had been listening to us. That look of effortless superiority I cultivate to hide my cringing soul had probably held them off until I departed, but they were wildly intrigued by the incongruity of my clothes with that look on my face. The shock of the hospital had driven away all my peasant posturing, needless to say.

They were both charming people, from St Andrews, and we moved over and joined them at their table. He was a newly retired professor of economics, Alan Boyd, and they were looking for somewhere warm and comforting where they could settle. After a lifetime in Scotland, they wanted the sun and had taken an apartment in the city for six months. He was a short, broad man with masses of crinkly grey hair, that he wore poetic and enjoyed. He was dressed like an exquisite; fawn, tapered linen slacks, a pale blue shirt and pale blue socks on sandalled feet. His hands were beautiful and carefully tended and so sexy they put you in mind of beds, like that – I'm afraid his teeth were false, but he didn't show them much, so I couldn't swear to it.

Unlike most academic wives – we have a university in Cardiff and I see a lot of them – his wife had kept her looks and her youth. Most academic wives look ten years older than their husbands, they struggle so hard to be the little handmaiden, helpmate, slave, they get to look like caricatures of denial. She hadn't. She'd been one of his students and still played the part, ingénue, artless, bubbling. Her hair was white and well styled, the eyebrows and lashes still very black and dramatised. Her tan was like a film star's and only the arms let her down. Arms are the acid test and there's nothing you can do about them. Margaret Boyd wasn't much over fifty but the backs of her upper arms had already that slack, flaccid lifelessness of old age. They hung like misplaced dewlaps above her elbows, crêpy, chicken-skinned, old.

We enjoyed them very much. We told them about the hospital and about my luggage and Joan produced the photographs of her children. I didn't have any of mine. I suppose it was significant of something – I wouldn't know.

They had a kind of intuitive knowledge that Joan was a Roman Catholic, as they were themselves. I imagine it's like being a Freemason, there must be signs. They talked about the Church and it was boring, small world stuff, about Sister this and Monseigneur that, small town gossip. Such a little world, the universal Church.

They called for another round but we were bored with slivovitz and they put us on to maraschino and on to the local gin. Then we called a round and they called another and it was lovely. A beautiful sticky haze, where hospitals and horrors and lost clothes, even lost stoles were just experiences, subjects of conversation, impersonal, removed.

It struck me that I was distinctly squiffy, even before lunch. My nonconformity shook a palsied finger at me. "For shame," I heard ancestral voices cry and felt impelled to say "Oh, isn't it awful! I'm a bit drunk, and before lunch at that. My mother'd be horrified. But she doesn't understand the restorative blessings of alcohol, how it cleans your eyes again. She wouldn't know, she's never tried."

"Never needed to, perhaps."

"Oh yes, goodness me, yes. Plenty of reasons, but she preferred religion. Hymns about the lowly Jesus and count your blessings. She had Jesus, she didn't need booze."

This left a kind of hiatus in the conversation. I felt I'd said something a bit wrong. They couldn't equate my non-conformist, lovely, sermon-on-the-mount mother with religion. For them she was misguided, foolish, wrong. A sinner indeed who had turned away from the light. We broke up then to go and eat, with promises to meet again. This was their pub, they were there every morning, we mustn't forget.

We couldn't face German conversation for lunch and decided to stay in the city and eat there. We found a restaurant and we ate red mullet and salad and had a bottle of white wine. A whole bottle for the two of us on top of what we'd already had, but it was so nice, so comfortable. Two waiters looked after us, it was late and the place nearly empty. We sat on a terrace shaded by vines and fed sparrows with breadcrumbs on the table. The sparrows made little droppings on the tablecloth, but we didn't care. And I never thought of the sparrows in London Airport, they were years away, that was in a far country and besides—

The waiters were friendly and practised their English on us and we were lazy and stupefied and happy and we didn't want to move. We paid our bill and overtipped and we loved everybody and then one of the waiters asked me, in Italian, as though it were a more suitable language, as indeed it was, whether we'd be interested in "cinque minuti" in their "camera" behind the restaurant. That theme again. What was this five minutes routine they had? I wasn't a bit cross this time, on the contrary, I was pleased that in spite of the black and everything, I'd had this invitation. These were personable young men, of course, that made one hell of a difference to the invitation. I had no intention of accepting it, Joan was unaware of it, she simply smiled benignly, slightly dazed about the eyes and I said "No, thank you. Not today. It's too hot."

I was pleased. I felt like a kitten. The waiters retired only slightly hurt and we went back to our hotel. On the way we remembered a piece of advice Alan Boyd had given us, that we should buy our own bottles of Scotch and English cigarettes at the duty free shops with our foreign currency. We should tank up in our own room rather than at the hotel bar. Quietly I'd thought that very decadent at the time, drink in the bedroom struck me as the first fatal step, but by then I didn't care and I'd tasted the local fags. So we shopped and then we slept, like two drunken sluts, and we smiled in our sleep.

I woke in the dusk of our untidy room, sober as Sunday, filled with hangover despair. I remembered the waiters and, bitter, I thought did they toss up in the kitchen for which one would have to take me? The black dress was hanging on the wardrobe door, like a bat, like death. I hated it. Where in the name of God was my suitcase, my clothes, all my things, what had I done to deserve this? Then I saw the bottle we'd bought. That was the answer, a quick nip before I was possessed. Mother naked, I pulled the cork and poured a dollop into the spare tooth mug. I had the first swig in my mouth when Joan opened one eye and said, "You don't know who's had their dentures in that glass."

I spat the whisky out like medicine. "What the hell's the point of having a bottle if we can't drink it? It's decadent enough having it in the bedroom at all, without being reduced to swigging it out of the bottle. There are limits."

"Pull something on you and away down to the bar for two drinks. Bring them up the stairs and we'll keep the glasses up here, out of sight."

I dragged on the hateful black dress again, sulky as an adolescent girl, resentful that I should be the one to go down, I don't much fetch and carry but for the duchess one did; it seemed perfectly acceptable. She was a treader but never made one feel much of a mat. I was cross then, but sober enough to know that with two hangovers in one small room, objections could be dangerous.

As I went through the door, she called out, "You might ask for a jug of iced water whenever you're about it. I don't trust these taps."

I collected the doings quickly wasting no time on strangled conversation with the barman, and mounted the stairs with dispatch. I was winded when I got to the first landing with my tray and stopped there to rest a minute. There was a big looking-glass on the turn of the stairs, one of those wicked ones with a flaw just where your face comes. My face looked back at me above that long black dress and I dodged a bit to get the flaw plumb in the middle. Now I had a nose and a half and my mouth had a swollen twist as if I'd had a nasty clout on it. My left eye was higher than the right one and my chin had receded to vanishing point. When I put my tongue out at me it was puffed up, monstrous. I was so like one of those obscene rubber puppets television inflicts on kids that I had to knock my drink back, quick, there and then, like any old alcoholic, before depression could twist its greasy fingers in my guts. In the sleeping corridor, I said aloud to my reflection, "I hate you. You're sordid, horrible, like a squashed fat spider on a cream-coloured wall. No, I'm wrong, on a pea-green wall. I'm on holiday, damn you."

Then I did my chimpanzee imitation and turned to go on to our room and saw Quasimodo, the night porter, watching me from the shadows.

Back in the bedroom I announced, "I'm damned if I'm going to appear for dinner dressed like this. Come on, shift, move out of that bed, we're going to buy me a dress in the city. I've had it."

But in the city there were no dresses I could buy. A dress that was slim enough for me came to well above my knees; in a dress the right length, I looked ten months pregnant. All I bought after all the fuss was a pair of blue nylon pants and a black leather belt which I fixed around my waist to pouch up the old maternity and make it that much shorter. It looked so contrived, I was like a rag bag.

We ate in the city again that evening. The dining-room in the hotel was so dressed up I felt I was an insult to it, felt I ought to apologise to the manager for letting his place down.

We had to find a new restaurant after the lunch-time proposals. That was two places, now, we'd have to avoid, the icons and that restaurant. We mustn't forget. We went to a busy place where the waiters had no time and where I was lost in the press, and in the warm dark afterwards the city was enchanting. The noise of people like starlings coming to roost, the lights on white marble streets that flowed like water, the ancient walls, encircling, eternal. We sat on the warm stone steps of the Cathedral watching the people and the pigeons strutting between us and the stage-set façade of the Renaissance Bishop's Palace across the way. It was like being a Capulet, but luckily it didn't strike me then that we two might have been mistaken for Juliet and the nurse. Not that Joan would really do for Juliet. As she'd said herself, keeping the secret of her age, "Sure, I'll not tear in the plucking" – but perhaps you don't know that in plucking the feathers of a young bird, it's hard not to tear the flesh. So few people do things like plucking any more; people campaign about battery hens and insecticides harming our insides, but they never complain about what this kind of non-activity does to our language. Language lives longer than us, poetic poverty is worse than dietary poverty, as long as you're not actually starving, I think, though who would dare say that to an Indian or a black African?

The two Boyds came and joined us on the steps – it was that kind of small city. You'd never be able to hide in it, not that we wanted to, mind you, except from the man in the icons and possibly the two waiters.

They insisted that we should walk home with them and we liked that and climbed up a gulf of fifty-seven steps to their apartment. The steps were old and crumbling, each flight barricaded, boxed, by the walls of tall houses on either side and each succeeding landing was the courtyard, backyard of the house above.

Their place had that cold, dominating, bossy atmosphere of most furnished accommodation abroad. Furniture designed to impress and intimidate and keep you in order.

Big things. Ornate sideboards like sarcophagi; hard, moralistic couches screaming Thou shalt not, artificial flowers arranged like immortelles on the grave-stone rigidity of high gloss. Nasty sentimental pictures and some cold Greek-looking plaques.

Margaret and Alan Boyd looked like two naughty children thumbing their noses at it, full of the devil and warm. They poured us drinks, made us welcome, confided about their financial problems and the job of keeping their landlady's cap straight.

But me – will you tell me, for heaven's sake, what's wrong with me? – I was constrained, a bit forced, falling over backwards to be at ease and never quite making it. I kidded myself it was because of the religion thing, they all had that world in common, had a bridge. I could talk economics; hell, I'd read it at the university, we had a world too. But you'd hardly compare the closeness of a shared religious experience with a half-remembered understanding of marginal utility and demand curves. Again, I would have preferred the prayers. That's another thing middle age does to you – softens your rejections, weakens your unconvictions; makes your basic premises, acceptances, assumptions as slack as the elastic in an old pair of directoire knickers, working-class – blue ones. There's something in me that's eroded all to hell, there's a shutter down and Jesus knows who's got the key.

The sight of me in that large, belted black dress moved the bowels of compassion in Margaret, thank God, and she offered to lend me some of her clothes. We were the same size; I must, of course I must. I didn't need much pushing, believe you me, and I posted to her bedroom with almost wicked speed.

Oh, the joy of clothes that clung, embraced, that fitted. It felt like the Birth of Venus, not that she's actually got any clothes on, but you know what I mean. A lovely, lovely female session in the bedroom, trying things on, talking clothes and where we shopped and had we seen that feature in *Harpers*? Nice to be women, nice to be soft. I was easier by then, two whiskies easier.

We left late, with two paper carrier-bags full of things for me. A day dress, a more formal black dress, some red pants, lots of blouses and even some bits of jewellery to wear with the formal dress. Baa, baa, black sheep, yes, sir, yes, sir, two bags full. It was far too late for the tram and we took a taxi. We were gay and excited, chattering the relief of Mafeking. We couldn't exclude the taxi-driver and we told him – in a terrible, polyglot, drunken conversation with sentences like "Haben sei bambini, drug?" – how much we loved his beautiful city and adored Yugoslavia and the sunshine was wonderful and yes, indeed, we loved slivovitz too. Joan was feeding me with suggested subjects and I did my tiddly best to translate and he did his best and we laughed a lot, not always at the same things. Then in a deserted, dark patch just short of our hotel, where they were putting up a new one, he stopped the car. He turned round to face me and in the starlight I saw that he was handsome, a big Slav face, strong, like a visiting diplomat and, would you believe it – it was cinque minuti again. Cinque minuti with la bella donna and there would be no fare.

"Non", I said, "niente". Joan had recognised the five minute routine and was laughing helplessly in her corner. "La donna è maritata, Cattolica. Sei bambini," I added for good measure.

"Sei bambini?" he snorted, "Dove bambini?"

"Bambini in Irlanda con il marito."

"Sei bambini con il marito?" Another incredulous snort, and really you could hardly blame him, could you – I mean what husband would stay at home with six babies? Certainly no good Slav.

"Solamente cinque minuti," he pleaded.

"Non. Io cappucio per il marito. Subito. Subito, per favore."

Joan wiped her eyes. "No," she said "no," and laughed aloud again. That laugh was more effective than all my protestations and six kids. No man, especially a Slav, likes his proposals laughed at. He slammed home his gears and drove on and we were very quiet in the back seat.

At the hotel gates, he turned again.

"Niente?"

"Niente!" I said and he overcharged us but we over-tipped, so we both won.

Quasimodo was on duty and insisted on taking us up in the little lift. He had no designs on Joan, only phantasies, but in spite of my little performance in the looking-glass that afternoon, he tried to get very close to me, only I had a carrier bag for padding and could breathe yet another prayer of thanksgiving to Margaret Boyd.

While we washed and undressed for bed and I hung up my beloved clothes Joan asked, "What's wrong with these men, at all? Haven't they wives of their own to satisfy them?"

"They feel they'd like a change, perhaps, and I guess we're asking for it, on our own without our men. Maybe they think we're looking for it and they're only fulfilling their patriotic duty offering tourist facilities."

"Away with you, woman dear, neither of us has got that hungry look. No, I'm thinking it's all these phallic symbols that's lying about, d'you know that?"

"Where?"

"Well, there's the clock tower, for a start, right in the heart of the city; there's all those wee turret things on the city walls, there's gargoyles about with their tongues sticking out, and look at the balconies, for crying out loud."

"You can't call a balcony a phallic symbol, not even in your wild Irish imagination. A balcony is flat, flat and square."

She started to laugh again then and fell on her back on the bed at the prospect of love with a balcony. "No, no, I mean those drain things that stick out of them for rain water. Wee spoutings."

"I haven't noticed them. I'm going to look."

"It's too dark, look in the morning. Hush, will you listen? I can hear a mosquito. God, will you look around the light? There's dozens, they'll have us killed."

Which indeed they did. They bit us to death, Joan had thirty-five bites on her back, I counted them for her. For a change of diet they'd gone for my legs and feet and I had to let my sandals out two holes for the swelling. When I woke that morning my legs and feet were on fire with bites and I was scratching in a frenzy. My maniac scratching brought home to me how right they were to tell you that scratching is rude, to equate it with nose-picking and what they call self-abuse. They're right, you know – apart from looking ugly and vulgar, scratching, for women anyway, is positively danger-ous unless you're home and happy and everything is fine. What I'm trying to say is that scratching is a form of sex – you begin with a gentle scratch that's not much more than a tickle and then it gets faster and you get sort of more involved with your scratching fingers, more part of them, they're not appendages, they're you. And then the frenzy begins and you scratch up to a climax and it's almost like an orgasm – it even has the same feeling of descent after the frenzy.

Those morning thoughts shot me out of bed and, to change the subject, I went to gloat again over my wardrobe. I had a tremendous kind of ritual wash before getting dressed, cutting my toenails, shaving my legs, plucking stray eye-brows, all the trimmings. Then I put on my new blue pants, my own good bra and petticoat washed the night before and still a bit damp in the elastic parts, and then I put on Margaret's little day dress. I wanted to be alone to assess it, like a child alone with a Christmas stocking, afraid of what might be wrong. The balcony was the place. Joan seemed to be asleep but she often slept like the butcher's dog.

Out there in the morning sunshine I enjoyed myself, I mean got joy from myself. The building labourers were down at ground level, I could see one of them lying on a plank in the shade, waiting for work to begin. His feet were bare, the soles towards me, calloused, splayed, ugly feet, but work-worn, honest feet. Old Renoir had something.

I looked at me. It was a little shift dress, cut straight, shaped only for the bosom. I'm a great believer in a good bra. What a splendid euphemism the advertisers have found in "foundation garments" – were they aware, I wonder, of the biblical connotations – not building your house on sand, building your house on a firm foundation. Such a comfort, firm breasts, oh yes. I feel much more naked without a bra than without knickers, don't you?

It was a little floral dress, not really me at all, soft and floral and muted, blues and mauves and a soft apple green. No, not me. It was light-hearted, easy, sort of Fern Hill. But I've never dared go floral and muted; tangerine, black, red, positive, uncompromising colours, checks and stripes, never flowers for me.

But I liked myself in this little floral wisp. I ought to wear scent with it, look floral, smell floral. But I never wear scent, never dared, not even those scents they call sophisticated, in case anyone should think I was sort of trying and being pathetic. Me and scent a sort of saddening little effort, like twittering, paper-thin, spinster aunties inventing lovers.

But this dress, it really asks for scent. Maybe I should try it. Lord, imagine my sixth form if I turned up soft and floral and muted and smelling of flowers. Well, after all, why not?

Funny about this dress, I almost feel it untying knots in me. It's only relief because it fits, really, I know, but what if it's telling me something? That the aggressive colours and positive clothes are really too big a burden to live with? That I should take it easy, be easy, let it go? It was lovely, like putting down two heavy shopping baskets that have left your hands numb and white and creased with weight.

"Where the hell are you at all?"

"Out here on the balcony."

"Are you decent? Is your man out there?"

"I'm perfectly respectable and he's down below taking a break. I came out to look at your phallic symbols," I lied.

"See what I mean?"

"God, yes, why ever didn't I notice them before?" And she was right. Damn right. I looked up at the façade of the hotel, white concrete, green shuttered, with a beard of Virginia Creeper up to the second floor. Each window had its concrete, fretted balcony and each indeed had its phallic symbol – a length of lead piping about a foot long that protruded in the lewdest way from one corner. Of course, once you begin thinking like this even the cypresses, I mean, there was something everywhere.

I turned my eyes away and concentrated on the Virginia Creeper that struggled up and piled over on to our balcony, that was safe at least. But no, those little, seeking, creeping tendrils were suddenly obscene; pinky little creeping sneaky fingers. Good heavens, it's the heat. I must go indoors.

CHAPTER 5

We met Franko on the steps of his agency. He had been out at the airport all night and now had some hours off. He wasn't only crucified-looking, you'd think he'd been laid in the tomb as well. His face was creased like an old working boot and his lids were drooping over the black eyes.

"What you need is a drink," Joan informed him, "Come on, come and have one with us and will you tell us what's happening to my friend's luggage at all?"

"I am desolate. There is no news. But now we think perhaps Zagreb. They searching Zagreb today."

"Well I don't think Zagreb. I think London. I mean, it's obvious, they took it off the plane and never put it back. For spite, for all we know."

"But, madam, you have clothes on you today. You are happy."

"Yes, I'm delighted, come on, let's go and celebrate the dress I borrowed. You do need a drink. You look awful."

It wasn't yet eleven o'clock in the morning and we were sitting drinking hard liquor in a café. And I couldn't pretend I was drowning any sorrows, hiding from anything. I was loving it. Oh booze, it is a blessed thing, beloved from pole to pole, it made me so nice, so easy. Drink and a dress. God bless everybody and me too.

Franko was telling us about his job and about the Yugoslav economy, explaining the problems of regionalism, how, say, one region couldn't have a motor car industry without giving one to the other four as well, so you couldn't hope to concentrate your industrial effort. About how wise President Tito had been to ignore the religious – it made a tremendous difference to the tourist trade. About there being no sex crimes in Yugoslavia Joan and I said "cinque minuti" in one breath and, like schoolgirls, hooked fingers and named poets.

"You must be very proud of the success of your country. Very happy."

"And living in this wonderful place. So beautiful, so warm."

"For my country, yes, I am happy, for myself it is not so."

"And Franko, why? What's wrong?" Easy, pub sympathy.

"See," he said, "see, how are my wrists. I slash them, so –" and he held out his hands to us across the drink-littered, cig-arette-strewn, sordid rickety little table and we saw two violent red scars across the delicate veins and bones of both wrists. "I was not happy. I did this thing, but it is easier to do such a thing if you are rich. To do it well you must have two things. You must have such a bath in which you can lie down and you must have hot water in your taps. This I do not have, I have only a basin and the water is cold and they find me and I am save."

"Oh no! but why?"

"It is my wife. She throw herself out of window and break her legs and I am desolate. Is my fault."

"What were you up to, at all?"

"I am Bosnian boy. You must understand this. We do not like only the one woman, all the time only one, and my wife she is jealous, she is not Bosnian, she cannot understand this thing. Perhaps I am bad boy, I don't know, but I am Bosnian. She knows this, but is no good for her."

"Oh Franko, I'm so sorry."

"And how many children do you have? Tell me that."

"No children. No."

"You give that girl of yours a few kids and you stay home and help her with them. I've no patience with your nonsense. None at all. Kids, that's the answer. God in heaven, with a handful of kids you'll be too tired for your fancy women and she'd have her hands too full to think of windows. You're wicked, so you are, d'you know that? And will you not get us another drink, Innes, what I had has turned sour in my guts."

But I was on his side. I put my hand on his scarred wrist. "I'm sorry, Franko. And is it over now?"

"Stop it, stop it, stop it." Joan yelled, slapping her hand down on the table till the glasses jumped and the tin ashtray skittered off. "I won't have it. It's all too real. You'll start her thinking again whenever she's only today stopped it. Now finish all this and start being cheerful again. You've got no business."

"Yes, madam, you are right. And I must go. I am very tired and must go to my bed."

Joan nodded her irritation at him. "Yes, that's right, go to bed and rest, but by yourself, mind. If you were a son of mine, I'd take your pants down, big as you are."

The aluminium teeth flashed a wavering smile at us, Joan's threat to take his pants down had confused him, not unnaturally, but he made us a low bow and walked away into the sunshine.

"Did ever you hear the like of that? He's like a walking wake; that's what thinking leads to, I warned you. You know, that dress is lovely on you. The colours do a lot for your eyes. It's nice. Away for those drinks now, like a lamb. We're wasting the sun, you know that?"

"Lovely way to waste it, though."

"Aye. It is surely, but we must get something for these bites and a spray, in case those bastards come in again the night. They close the shops before we come awake here."

At the apotek they recommended camphorated oil in little plastic bottles for our bites and told us where to buy an aerosol for the mosquitoes. Next door to the chemist was the perfumery and we went in there too and bought scent. She was an Arpège girl and here it was duty free and I bought something French that suited my dress, but bore no relation to me or what I thought I was.

How easy it was to be happy, all I needed was a dress and a few drinks, and there was no "kybe of conscience" to put me to my slipper, nothing but mosquito bites.

We spent the afternoon writing picture postcards on the beach. Wish you were here with us, we wrote, and looked at each other.

"Do you, honestly? Tell the truth and shame the devil."

"No, not really. Do you?"

"No. Will you listen to me. There's no ba crying for me, there's no kids quarrelling in my ears, there's no neighbours, nobody's watching my health and counting my drinks."

"And there's nobody thinking you're better than you are. No bloody pedestals set on other people's standards."

"Christ, pedestals. They kill you, don't they? There's times when the love and the dependence of them chokes me. There's only me and seven of them, himself's the worst. Milking me and me with dry udders."

"Who's thinking now, duchess, be careful. But, Lord, I know what you mean. They're missing us now like having a leg off or something and assuming, of course, that we're missing them as much. Trusting us to miss them. But we're not and I don't care and it's lovely and thank God it was you in the other bed."

"Oh, they're nice, too. I wouldn't be without them, but the break's just fine, so it is."

"And think, if we weren't loved, if they weren't there. If only one could be loved for what one is, not what they've made us. That's too much to ask for, though. 'Only God, my dear, could love thee for thyself alone and not thy yellow hair.' My yellow, yellow hair is as much a fake as the rest of me."

"Get on with your cards, now, or we'll be home ourselves before they arrive."

"And if mine doesn't get word from me soon he'll start to fuss and send telegrams."

"Oh, I know, I'll tell you what's wrong with our men. They're too nice. They don't give you a chance, do they? Forgiveness and understanding and never a bloody good fight. Here, your back's red, let me put a bit more of this stuff on it. How am I?"

"You could do with a bit, too. Tell you what's wrong, this stuff doesn't want to mix with the camphorated. Thank God we've got that spray for tonight."

"We may make sure those bits of mosquito wire are fixed as well. Does my back look awful?"

"Well, it's got thirty-five bites on it and just look at my legs."

"The bastards. But we'll fix them tonight. Must send a card to Reverend Mother. Have you got a nice Goddy one there? I couldn't send her the beach and bikinis, God help her. Remind me to find an artistic, religious one for Monseigneur tomorrow. We should have got a few of those icon ones, you know that?"

"Well, we're not going back for those, my love, not even for his Holiness himself."

"No, fair enough. Sure, if he saw you dressed he'd have you raped, so he would. Will you wear the black dress tonight?"

"Yes, why not? I've my own good shoes."

The black dress was a little flared number, with a deep frill around the low neck and three-quarter sleeves. I would never have as much as tried it on in a shop, frilly and feminine, the neck-line demanding young skin and a pretty face that it could frame. But I saw and smelled myself in it through a thin haze of Scotch, put on my superiority look and blew smoke down my nose at my reflection.

As we passed the bar, we were hailed by five female bodies from Glasgow; delighted to see me pansied up at last, they would stand us a celebratory drink. We talked tourist till they left us to go, in pink and blue lace dresses, to some high jink or other. We hadn't finished our drinks when Joan realised she'd come without a handkerchief and, like an arch-duchess now, she left the bar to go back to our room.

I was leaning on the bar and watched the barman watch her go. He was a big, white-haired Slav, white-coated, polite, dignified and typical of the average Yugoslav, in whom ser-vility never arises, in whom equality and fraternity is the expected, accepted attitude. He watched her out of sight, his eyes full of wonder, softened with delight, then he caught me watching him and was disconcerted, shamed.

"Bella donna, si?" I said.

"Ah," he murmured, with a deep, deep sigh. "Bella donna? Prima bellisima donna," and he poured us both another drink and we clicked our glasses and downed it, only just restraining ourselves from throwing the glasses over our shoulders.

Our table was empty when we arrived and we encouraged Blado to serve us quickly, to save us from the awful embar-rassments of German conversation. But we were only tucking in to our Wiener Schnitzels when the Germans arrived, gracious and charming and silent. We greeted them and smiled and Joan pointed to her watch and ate fast and indicated a great hurry. And they understood and waved tol-erant hands and we pitched in, but as soon as our plates were cleared, there we were, once more, silent, defenceless. Not even the black dress and the scent were enough to give me the confidence to shut up.

I went and remembered the phrase "Gute Fahrt", a good journey, which the kids had laughed at so much in Germany and, a bit tiddly, I thought I'd be clever. It's always a mistake. I had a half sort of memory that if you added "ge" to the beginning of some nouns, you could form a verb and I decided that gefahrtten probably meant something like go on a journey. Brightly, and would-be sophisticate, in black, I said "Ich denk Sie gefahrted haben."

I'd wanted to say I thought you'd gone on a journey, on an expedition, were away for the day, sort of thing, because they were late. Only God knows what I did say. I've never dared enquire. But whatever it was, it was mad. Joan was convinced I'd accused the man of farting and her tears were streaming. The Germans first looked embarrassed and then the little woman caught Joan's eye and began to heave with laughing. The man caught the infection, he may have known a few English four-letter words, for all I know, and he grinned all over his face and turned to the next table and told our neighbours what I'd said and everybody laughed. Big teeth, big noises. I felt mobbed. I was ready to die, blushing and trying to be dignified and too mad with myself to laugh and not knowing what the hell I'd said. Oh it was shameful. I can laugh now, but then – my pride nearly choked me, honest. I'm so bad at laughing at myself. Pretend to, of course, make a big joke of my misfortunes, dine out on them. You've got to, to live with them, but not to yourself; you do it to take out the public sting, but is it possible to take out the private sting? Not for me it's not.

That finished me for the meal. I'd made my contribution to harmony and universal brotherhood and all they got out of me after that was "Gute Nacht" and out.

Out was to a café across the road where they sang folk songs to an accordion. It was more like a garage than a café, really, in fact I think it may have been a garage until quite recently. It smelled a bit like that. It would have held one car and a few bikes, but now the walls were white-washed, there were benches around the walls and tables and a bar counter to one side. It was pretty full when we came up to the door and they were singing "We shall overcome" so we went in and got a few inches on a bench with them. There wasn't much shape to the singing and they sang the strangest mixtures of time, place and sentiment. Fancy singing "Lily Marlene" in Yugoslavia, for example, but, of course, that may have been, like cinque minuti, a tourist attraction. They sang "Pack up your Troubles" and "Tipperary" and "Auprès de ma blonde" and the "Volga Boatmen" in what we took to be Russian and their own songs, lots of them dirty, I suspect, from the bawdy looks and the guffaws.

We were sitting on this long bench thing by the wall but there was a deal of coming and going and we got a bit more room and then we moved up for others coming in and somebody stood us a drink and then we ordered a round for the table and it was like all pubs and the singing made most of the conversation. The man sitting beside Joan was a middle-aged man with cadaverous, hollow cheeks, gold fillings in all his front teeth and big, sad, brown eyes. He spoke quite good English in between songs and said he lived in Austria. His name was Adolf, if you please. Couldn't think why he hadn't changed it. He said he wouldn't bother us with his other name because it was Polish. Then the chap on my side began talking to me. His English was laboured, but he persevered like mad and, fair play, why shouldn't he practise his English on me? I rather enjoyed talking to him and putting in the odd correction, he reminded me a bit of my elder son and that was nice. He was only a boy, but he did give me one piece of good linguistic advice. I'd been making tremendous efforts to address men as "drug" – comrade – but it hadn't always seemed to be quite the thing. And this boy told me why. "Drug" tended to be used only by one party member to another and one should say "gospod" – sir, gentleman – rather than "drug". That rather shook me, but I thought it might have been the reason for some of our invitations. Perhaps "drug" could mean a term of endearment, somehow.

Across the table from us was a very drunken man who kept waving his glass under our noses and saying "Chinchin". I didn't want to offend him – you know how drunken men can be – so I put out my hand and said "Innes" and he shook my hand with courtly, plastered dignity and then he kissed it. He turned to Joan and again he said "Chinchin" waving his glass at her. "Introduce yourself," I said, "he's telling you his name is Chinchin or something."

"Lunatic," she whispered, choking, "he's saying 'Chin chin,' like cheers, say it back to him before he drowns you with your glass."

"Oh," I said, brightly "Yes, indeed, chin chin, Good health."

"Chin chin" he said again, and "Edinburgh," and slipped slowly under the table, spilling most of his drink on my good shoes.

Meanwhile the boy had been playing with my fingers, admiring my engagement ring, and turning my palm up, he pinched it quite hard and said "Soft, you not work hard."

"No, I'm a teacher." I felt a bit soft, not liking to pull my hand away and yet not liking to have it held like that and pinched. It hurt, for a start. Then I thought to reach for a cigarette and they all appreciated my English ones and the boy lit mine and in the lighting moved up much closer to me, almost snuggled into me, but, as I said, he did remind me a bit of my son and the bar was crammed.

"You have a lovely stink," he said into my left ear.

"No, no, not stink, smell. We say stink for a bad smell," and I held my nose to illustrate. "Stink is bad, smell is good.

"You have a lovely smell?"

"Yes."

"A lovely smell. In here is not so good for you. The lovely smell is besser outside, no?"

"Perhaps." I thought he was still practising his English and wasn't weighing my answers.

"Come, we go. Cinque minuti, we come back." I promise you, he was a little boy, twenty-two at most. "Don't be silly," I turned schoolmarmish, "I like it here."

"But we come back. Only five minutes."

"Look, I have a son as old as you and I'm not interested, understand?"

"But madam, Oedipus is goot, too." Would you believe it? It must have been the sun and those symbols.

"No, thank you" I said and kicked Joan on the ankle. "It's the old routine," I told her, "we'll have to beat it."

"Jesus, not again? Not with thon wee one?" I nodded my eyes and we got up and said Goodbye very graciously and her Adolf got up too and said he would see us to the hotel. My boy glowered at me and I said "Dovegnia, gospod" to show I'd learned my lesson, if he hadn't.

Adolf walked with a limp and wore lederhosen and the lights from the café shone harshly on several great scars across his thighs. He was ashamed of his limp, I think, and quickly explained that he'd been wounded in the war, that his was a worthy limp, not a physical deformity.

I asked him where he'd seen action. My Mike had been in the R.A.M.C. and I knew what to ask a soldier.

"It was on the Russian front. That you will know was a bitter place." There was a kind of pride in his voice. Polish name, living in Austria, on the Russian front. What was he?

"Were you fighting with or against the Russians?"

"I was in the German army." There was no keeping the pride out now, he straightened his back, held up his head. That finished me. I'm wickedly unforgiving to the Germans. I know it's bad, but there it is, apart from all the other horrors they stole six years of my marriage, our six first years when we were in love and young and lonely. I grudge them my six young years as well as the six million.

I made no response to Adolf. We came to the hotel door and I went quickly for the key in case he offered to shake hands with me. I heard his "Good nights" and then Joan's cheerful "Till tomorrow, then".

I rounded on her. "What d'you mean, till tomorrow? You're not going to see that swine again."

"Of course we are" she said blandly, mounting the stairs ahead of me. "Sure, he's nice and he's someone to talk to. I'm sorry for him, with that limp and all."

"Sorry for him? You heard where he got the limp? On the Russian front and he has the face to come here to Yugoslavia."

"Och away with you, woman dear, it's ancient history. We'll talk to him tomorrow and you'll see for your own self. You'll like him. I know you will You're the one talks about toleration. You don't know the meaning of it."

"Speak for yourself, sister, I'm having nothing to do with him." I unlocked the door and put on the lights. "And since he's so proud of his old German Army, what's he doing living in Austria with his old Polish name? He's one of the S.S. he is, I'm sure of it, hiding in Austria with a bogus identity he's probably stolen from some poor bastard in a concentration camp and those gold fillings are horrid as well."

"Shut up, shut up, can you hear a pinging? They're in here again. Where's that spray thing? Where the hell did we put it?"

"I know. It's in the wardrobe, we hid it with the glasses. Move, for me to get it."

"Shh. Now, don't disturb them, they haven't noticed us yet. See them, there's four on the wall in that corner and would you look around the light?"

"Here it is. Here goes." I was standing on a chair to reach the top shelf of the wardrobe and from that eminence I aimed our spray at the cluster by the light. The tin flew out of my hand like a firework and landed on the floor between the two beds, whirling and spitting and sizzling. Joan leapt on it and tried to press the plunger to stop it, but there was no stopping it. It spun in her hand, covering her face and clothes with stinking fly-killer. She flung it back at me and the sides were now all slippery and impossible to hold. It got me in the eye and, blinded, I chucked it back again where I expected her to be. You couldn't see across the room, even with two eyes, and you couldn't breathe at all. We rushed for the window and stopped. No, there were more of them out there queuing up to come in, so we rushed the door and poured out, but Quasimodo was out there, lurking, and we bounced back in again. The tin was still spitting and sputtering like a bad-tempered snake on the floor and spinning, thrashing around with its own fury. Unleashing the anger of that thing was worse far than mosquitoes, it was a swarm of hornets, armed. We stood up on our beds above the worst of the miasma and there were the mosquitoes indifferently cleaning their wings for supper. The spray was quieting down to a small, sullen, frustrated hiss and then it gave a sob and fell over and died.

We can't sleep in this, you know that? It'll poison us – there's been books about it."

"But where can we go? The bar and everything's closed. There's only the lav."

"O.K. We'll leave the door open to air this place and go in there. For Pete's sake don't forget the air freshener. There's your man, Quasimodo. What's he thinking, I wonder? If he sees us going into the lav together, he'll have us down for two lesbians."

"Who cares? It'll put him off."

CHAPTER 6

I'll tell you one of the best places for being along and safe from sympathy or seduction – a cemetery.

When, bitchy but adamant, I abandoned Joan to her Adolf next morning, I took myself off to the local cemetery. Franko had told me the way to it, and that "Today they search in Split". Nobody bothers you in a graveyard, they respect your grief or your meditation or whatever it is you've come for. To be solitary in a cemetery is proper and nearly always safe.

There was no room in that enclosed city for the dead, they lay outside, on the terraced mountain. I climbed there by the back streets of the city, up hundreds of steps, through courts and colonnades, passed the back door of one house and, on the same level, the stork-like chimneys of the next; by the upstairs balcony of this and the wine cellar of that, by the still, calm Virgin in her niche over a door, and a mule stock still in a moment of shade. Old houses, mellow with ripe apricot walls or crumbling white-wash; old ladies sat at doorways, in their black, and called to each other, in black head-scarves and dresses and black plimsolls.

But even on the hillside there wasn't much room for the dead; good land is too precious and the vines grew up to the very walls of the cemetery. So they'd put the dead into cavities within the walls, and when those were full, then more walls within walls were built up, with empty, yawning maws waiting for the next victim. The empty holes lying in wait and murmuring like an obsequious grocer, "And the next, please?"

I liked my walk, liked seeing without having to comment; I remember, appreciate so much more when I'm alone and undistracted and there's nobody wondering why. And here at last were the dead in their walls and in their enclosure there was no one, no one but me and the very dead and the lizards in the sun. It was silent there in the sunshine, but never still, the haunt of lizards. Beautiful little greeny brown lizards and fatter, greener, less friendly lizards that climbed all over the marble grave walls, quick and sudden as a spurt of fear; like monkeys with prehensile fingers gripping, groping in the "requiescat", picking a way through the "pace".

You're made so much more aware of the dead abroad with the photograph of its occupant on every tomb and the eyes that state their accusation at you. Remember me.

I wonder how the mourners decide on the picture that will truly represent their dead, what stage on the journey should they choose? The first communion innocence, the bridal insipidity, maternity, the middle prime or the declining threat of senility? What would one choose for oneself? When was oneself? This is the old problem that used to haunt my believing childhood. How would people look in heaven? I remember when my auntie died and me wondering whether, when I saw her again, she'd look like the gentle old lady I loved, who used to make bread and smell of baking and would let me pick out the dried dough from underneath her worn, broad wedding ring when I sat on her lap and we watched the flames and waited for the bread to be ready. Or would she look like the young one of her framed wedding-day picture whom I didn't know at all?

I sat on the edge of an empty tomb, the marble like silk to my fingers and a tall, thin cypress pointing beside me. I thought of the Lawrence poem and looked away, over to the mountain and there was such a village, eternal, inevitable. It was as if it had never been built, but had grown there, like an outcrop of rock, like a waterfall, natural as a tree. A few houses clustering the untidy fringes of the Church which was still the meaning and the purpose of the village. The church stood starkly white against the shifting greens of vine, olive and pine, a beacon, the pointing finger of authority, firm in

its antique posture. Say what you like, Franko, the church
remains, more than a tourist attraction – here I sit, your unbe-
liever, overawed and humble and begging for direction. But
you don't go screaming to the church, like a child to its mum,
because you've lost your way for a while. That would be
blasphemy and Joan's answers are too easy, anyway.

The lovely, lonely silence seemed to pour through me,
stroking me, knitting me up. I felt strangely mature, as
though the empty grave on whose edge I sat was an analyst's
couch. I could look at myself and not find myself entirely
wanting. I had a mood of charity, even to me, of temporary
clarity, I had a moment of faith that it would come back, that
I would be restored. The cemetery was Cythere and something was promised me.

"Ah Seigneur! donnez-moi la force et le courage
De contempler mon coeur et mon corps sans dégout."

When I rejoined Joan for lunch at the hotel I was gay, as if
I'd been spending a lot of money on clothes, as if I'd been
shopping with my daughter or watching cricket with my sons
or been making love to Mike in the middle of the afternoon
out of doors. Joan was less pleased with her Adolf now, not
for my sort of reasons, they were almost irrelevant to her, but
because he'd been talking about his "problems" and telling
her about his analyst. Joan dismissed "problems" merely as
failures of common sense. She had no sympathy to spare for
neurotic behaviour. If a child was difficult you reasoned with
it, if that failed you beat it and sent it to confession. Adults
should have more sense, psychological weakness she considered madness. Fair enough, I suppose. Anyway, she'd lost
sympathy with her Adolf. She wrote him off – "Sure, he's like
a pair of those hair clippers that'll neither cut, pull nor let go."

I didn't tell her about my cemetery. She would have
laughed and it was still precious, though the special feel of it,

the secret, was already slipping fast into the light of common day. Faced with a good meal and a bottle of wine I was already a bit ashamed of having gone in for what in Wales we call "Walocs". It's not really translatable because it's an attitude which is specially Welsh. The word isn't even literary Welsh, you won't find it in Welsh books – the people who use it don't write books. Writing books might even be part of it. It's a mixture of affectation, pretentiousness, posing, whimsy, would-be-ness making a performance, a parade of notions, of sentimentalities. It's the opposite of plain common-sense, bitter realities, simplicities, honesties. It's an unsympathetic, perhaps insensitive word, but it's solid, rooted, touchstoned.

In that morning's solitude, whether it was walocs or a sort of donation or simply what Joan called thinking, I had escaped, escaped from the holiday and the holiday person I was required to be, easy, lazy, loosed. The cemetery was a back-sliding, disloyal to her and the pattern of this time. She'd asked for laughter and I'd gone and hidden myself among the tombs. It was like quoting from the *Inferno* or using Hieronymous Bosch in a sea-side brochure. Plain daft. But I'd liked it and there was no need to confess.

We went by motor boat to an island that afternoon. A small, thickly wooded island where there were the ruins of a Cistercian monastery and the decayed splendours of a great house. Now it was a public place; there was a café and bathing off the yellow-lichened rocks, a harsh place, but beautiful, with pines and olives, rough seagrass and pinks, prickly, and with ants and negligent bits of Ancient Rome in the ruins and along the marble paths.

Joan had spent her morning with Adolf. He'd been drinking, in a manic frenzy for words, punctuating paragraphs with slivovitz and every sentence with cigarettes. She had had to drink to keep awake and was not quite at her soberest. Settled and oiled on the island rocks, we tried to read for a while but she couldn't come to terms with Miss Compton-Burnett and I had long since tabled a note of no confidence in my Prime Minister. Then Joan, cross-legged and dogged, decided to tidy out her handbag. Bus tickets from Ballyduggan to Belfast, thick and sweet with spilt powder, bills from the butcher, the baker and the wee woman down the road, large blue safety-pins, rosary beads, a baby's dummy-teat with a bedraggled blue bow, Arpège, lumps of soiled 100 dinar notes, a passport containing hairgrips, her air ticket, driver's licence and her purse.

The bills and the bus tickets she folded up together in a thick wad and stuffed them firmly down into a crevice in the rock. "They'll see the colour of my money when it suits me. They may thank God I took their bills on holiday for them, so they may."

She kissed the dummy teat and popped it into her mouth and sucked loudly, oblivious to the incredulity on the faces of a gaggle of Germans sitting near us. When she tired of this comfort she turned to her purse and shook all the English and Irish coins out of it and into the cave, the crotch of her crossed legs. There was a lovely rich, round rattle as they poured out, bouncing and rolling on the hot rocks. She slapped her hands on the rolling ones and gathered the lot into a miser's hoard in front of her. First, with careful concentration she sorted out her copper ones and dropped them solemnly, deliberately, into holes in the rocks. Then she saw an old tin and aimed the last copper ones at that and never a bull's eye. Worthless old British coins. The hell with them. The last ones she simply threw up over her head and watched them roll away over the rock and into the sea and she clapped her hands to see them go.

The dead had offered me only communion wine so I soberly wrote a letter to Mike. It wasn't a sober letter, though, it was a lovely letter and I knew he'd go crazy to get it. A happy, articulate, close letter, to make him laugh, to make him want me, to make him know things were well with me – not a word about my luggage. A letter that matched my dress. I told him about Joan, about the phallic symbols, about the trees and the antiquities, the cemetery, the icons, even the teeth, and I told him how much I wanted him, wanted his body, not his presence, he wouldn't fit. I was more or less honest. I told him how in this sun and with no nightie I was aching for him, open and empty, and when I came home I'd eat him, gobble him. I knew he'd love my letter. I imagined the delight there'd be on his face as I finished it and addressed the envelope and put it into my handbag to wait for a post office and the right kind of stamp.

Joan complained that I was far too sober, and sure, wasn't there a bar on the island, what were we about at all?

At the next table to us there was a stoutish young man, very formally dressed with a tie and dark jacket and an exhibition blue handkerchief neatly folded in his breast pocket. He had a thick fall of young sun-bleached hair and his profile from where we sat was quite beautiful. We wished we were younger in spite of his stoutness. He looked as if he was about to go to his office. All he needed was a bowler and a briefcase and we wondered idly why he sat there so incongruously, so formally. Even as we looked he suddenly burst out laughing, loud uninhibited laughter, on his own. He took a letter out of his pocket and began to read it out loud, and the frustration was terrible because we couldn't understand a word of it and we died to know.

He read it to the end, four pages, and then he threw back his head and laughed some more, rocking back and forth on his chair like a pendulum and staring at the pages in his hand. Then with slow, mad deliberation, he took a box of matches, failed to strike the first few matches and then one caught and he lit a corner of his letter, lit each page and waved them in the heat haze and still the laughing and concentration and us watching like two frightened rabbits.

"Is your man mad at all?" she whispered.

"Bonkers."

"Move. Come on, we're away. If you look sympathetic I'll kill you, so I will. I've had a morning of it. Will you shift, woman."

"You don't think we should – "

"What in the name of God could we do? The man's a foreigner."

"No, I suppose not." And we went and we queued for the little motor boat that came bouncing towards us with its royal blue bright canopy and we left him, but what would you? When we landed on the marble of the quay we filled our mouths with talk and alcohol to wash him out, but we couldn't scrub him out of our minds, and then we saw an advertisement for a symphony concert that night and we grabbed at its promise and said, We'll do that. It'll comfort us. And wouldn't the husbands approve?

Dressed up to the nines, smelling like flower gardens or whores and only slightly unsteady on heels that seemed to have lengthened several inches, we arrived at the city gates to go to the concert. We both felt tremendously tall, first because of the business of the heels and then there were our stiff necks, held rigid with drunken dignity and the fact of going to the concert, the snob value of it making us arrogant and superior. Joan had cultivated a sort of rubric since the afternoon. Getting back to the hotel to change and eat had meant hurrying but Joan was impervious, imperious to time. What had drunken duchesses to do with the petty irritations of clocks and measuring, the concert would wait, she was coming. Whenever I nagged, for I am fundamentally humble, she said, "Don't rush me, Innes, don't rush me." She would wave her hands, the diamonds flashing, look helpless and dogged, the blue eyes glazed, the dignity complete, the articulation most carefully controlled and as English county as Ballyduggan permitted. "No Innes, don't rush me. I will not be rushed."

But rushed or not, we got to the city gates and I remember how it was there, all black and white and Byronic. White walls, black shadows and us in black dresses walking arm in arm down the white marble staircase and the balustrades beside us. I trailed one white hand negligently on the silken balustrade, dreaming drunk dreams of elegance and antiquity and courage and beauty, and suddenly the duchess tripped and fell flat on her arse in the middle of the steps.

"Christ," she said, "do you think I'm a trifle full?" still sitting there in her black chiffon and looking up at me, surprised. "But don't rush me, now, don't rush me. Just give the loan of your arm a minute."

"You are plastered, duchess, but plastered."

"Never been plastered in my life. Sure you've only got to swallow a lump of butter before you start the drinking and you'll never be stoned."

"Maybe you forgot the butter."

"Och, well, maybe I did. Well, come on, you may give me your arm."

"Upsidaisy."

"Upsibloody-buttercup. You know, it isn't me at all, it's these effing heels, so it is." But still she didn't move and the people walked around her and probably wondered.

"Let's take them off. Take your shoes off."

"Nonsense, Innes, one can't go barefoot in black."

"We can. We're special. Come on, let's take them They're killing us, anyway." I sat down on the steps her and still the people passed and swerve it was funny, in a forest of legs and dangl could see close, like Gulliver, see the s hairs on them erect in the lights, see th and the deformities of feet. Joan and I ings.

Arm in arm again we made the steps cobbled street, the cobbles warm and rou

the lights in them. "Look, look, it's Venice, marble water.
Paddle your feet in the cobbles. Lovely watery cobbles, curl
your toes round them. Feel them."

"You know something? You're stoned too."

"I didn't fall down the steps, whatever."

"Whatever," she echoed me, in a travesty of a Welsh
accent. "Whatever, indeed to goodness. I hate the bloody
Welsh, you know that? Want to make anything out of it?"

"You go to hell, I hate the bloody Micks too. Come on, for
God's sake, don't stand there measuring up. We'll miss this
concert. I know we will."

"Don't rush me, Innes, why do you always rush me?"

The concert was in the Bishop's Palace and they sold the
tickets in a portico supported by great pillars. As I waited for
my turn, I looked up into those pillars, into the capitals and
the vaulting. There's no doubt about it at all, you know, if
you have drink taken you are in easily the best state for
appreciating detail. Had I been sober waiting for those tickets
I'd have fussed and waited irritably, but then I was easy,
composed, gave my proper attention to the intricacies of the
capitals – to the leaves and flowers there, the mythological
animals, the mediaeval motifs and the children's games.
Lovely, light-hearted things, beautiful as a summer's day
when you were young and your mother.

After the portico, the square courtyard with colonnades
nd it and a great baroque staircase soaring up to the
ky. We sat in the colonnades and the orchestra in the
with the drums tucked under the sweep of
they were tuning their instruments and
aratory rustle of programmes and settling
and the habitués had their air cushions.
front row and it was going to be wonder-
ethoven and some Slav neither of us had
didn't know quite what they would play
mme was in Serbo-Croat, but it didn't

matter, it had to be wonderful. In such a setting, such a place and everybody dressed for it.

The conductor came and bowed and he was very pretty, a bit too pretty, I thought, for Beethoven, with his careful hair and languishing hands, more a Hollywood lover really than a Yugoslav conductor. He should have been more rugged, more a resistance than a romantic figure, but since they played Eine Kleine Nacht Musik first that was all right. It was just his cup of tea. Then it was the Emperor Concerto and the pianist was a wee, wee man from Czechoslovakia, bald as a plate, with glasses and the bouncy walk of confident little men. By the beginning of the second movement a terrible thing happened to me. I was dying to sleep, but dying. There in the front seats, the best seats, the orchestra was shimmying before me as if I was seeing them over the top of a hot stove in chapel. It wasn't only the disgraceful feeling of shame, it was torture as well, like rheumatism behind the eyes, like synovitis in the heart of you. I'd shake myself and make my back straight and think I was awake, only to find myself jerking into awareness and shame. I concentrated on the pianist's hands, on the thumps and the hammerings, but the noise wasn't making any sense, it was as if I'd slipped below music and no pattern was left. It was like trying to follow a knitting pattern in Russian. We were sitting almost at the feet of one of the double-bass players and I willed myself to watch him. He was making tremendous faces. A little man, again, cherubic with fat little baby's bum cheeks and a thick, highly mobile lower lip with which, I promise you, he was conducting. His legs were much too short to reach the floor and he had his feet planted, fat, on an old wooden box that had once contained tinned tomatoes; that was like the flowers on the balconies homely and unpretentious, but it wasn't enough. He was too close perhaps, his lower lip too like a metronome; I should look a bit further away, at somebody that required a bit more effort to watch. I picked on a flautist with flaming red hair and a Glasgow face, left over from the war. You'd have thought any girl would have had the sense to take precautions against that sort of stamping, dominating red hair, wouldn't you, but there he was, his keelie's face alight and serious. He kept me conscious for perhaps five minutes and then I jerked again, a big painful jerk that shook me and must have echoed along the whole front row. If only I could have lighted a fag, but the listening was so complete, a striking match would have been sacrilege. What was sleeping then? Sleeping in the Beethoven, what would I do for the Slav? Snore, no doubt. What if I'd snored already? I don't think I snore, not unless I've got a terrible cold, but with drink on me, you simply wouldn't know. There's so few people you can trust about snoring, husbands are too kind to say, mostly.

I gave in after the flautist failed, rested my head on my hand and let it go and then there was the clapping and I woke and joined in, all sly. I still don't know who that Slav was, nor what he had to say. I was asleep at the first bar and I can only take the duchess's word for it that I didn't snore. But the horror of waking up in public, the shock of it, the naked emptiness, the defencelessness, the chill, the exile and ignorance.

Joan was awake and critical. She dismissed the Slav and talked musical technicalities with a sophistication that left me humbled and completely surprised.

"Are you a musician, then?" I asked, amazed. "Do you play?"

"Yes, I play the piano, but not the sort of thing you'd appreciate, you old moo. Sleeping like that, I was ashamed of you, so I was."

"It was only for the Slav," I lied, "you didn't like him either."

"But where's your manners, woman?"

"Oh, I know. But I couldn't help it. It's all this drink, honest, it was the drink. Why does it have to be so cheap here? But don't mark me down, please don't mark me down."

"Jesus, chuck the guilt. Don't give me that. Why the hell you can't accept yourself for what you are I'll never know. You've got limitations, just like the rest of us, God knows, plenty of them; all this guilt crap is nothing but bloody pride. It's not a pretty face you're short on, it's plain honest humility. Now for heaven's sake come for a drink. You've slept yourself sober like an old sow and I've listened the drink away. We'll just have a wee night cap, just a drop of oil to soothe the bearings. And you be nice, now, be nice. Don't spoil the music for me."

But the wee night cap only served to churn up the booze that was floating around already, we'd neither slept nor listened it away and when we left our pub the drink had us captured again, willing, delighted captives, plastered, two drunken duchesses out on the cobbles, barefoot.

"I must spend a penny" she announced. "Find me somewhere. There's never a ladies in the place."

"Don't you dare do it on these cobbles. Not on these lovely cobbles." I threatened her with my shoes.

"Well, find me somewhere," she pleaded, holding herself like a small girl, her legs crossed.

"Don't hold yourself like that, people are watching you, and you in black and all. Let's get off this main street and we'll find a nice dark alley somewhere and I'll like hold the door. Did you have a best friend in school to hold the lav door for you?"

"Always. Always somebody to hold the door," and we turned up the nearest side street. It was a steep street, steep and dark, already mysterious, closed. Soon we were climbing steps and Joan, twisted to contain her bladder, was clinging on to the iron rail let in to the house walls. The steps climbed up and up, between the tall houses, with their balconies and their flowers and some with old family crests rebuking us. One feeble light pinpointed a balcony where dark flowers rioted down the miniature pillars.

"Look," she said, "purple flowers. Hate purple flowers. If you're around when they come to bury me, don't let them put purple flowers. Promise me." She stopped under the light, her face white with drink, drawn with the need to convince me, her body contorted around her bladder. "And I'll tell you another thing. In Ireland they put you in a brown shroud. That's another thing. Don't let them put me in a brown shroud. I want to go in white. You see to it. Promise. Go on, promise."

"O.K. I promise. If I'm still here, I promise."

"Jesus, Mary and Joseph, where can I go?"

"Look, there's another road at the top of those steps, there'll be somewhere up there. Don't stop here, they could still look up from the big street and there's this light as well. Can you make it?"

"I can but try."

At the top of the steps there was another street, narrower, darker, the houses poorer, with dark, arched caverns on the ground floors, like the stables they have in Italian villages.

"Duck into one of those. There may be a mule in there but he'll be company for you. Give me your shoes."

She crept, humbled, into the dark arch and I stood guard outside with my back to her. I heard the trickle of her and then a warm stream hit my stockinged feet and I rounded to avoid it and it was then I saw the light coming down some steps behind the duchess. There were two bare feet on the steps and then the bottom of a white nightgown. In the little light I saw that Joan's lavatory wasn't a stable at all, but somebody's front porch and that somebody was coming down to investigate.

"Will you for God's sake hurry."

"Don't rush me, Innes, don't rush me."

"Somebody's coming after you. It's her front porch

you're in. Come on, will you? Run. I'm off. She'll have our lives."

"Oh Jesus save us, Holy Mary, Mother of God—"

"There's no time for prayers. Run. For Pete's sake, run. She can't come far after us in bare feet and a nightie. Get down the steps."

The nightdress was calling after us now, we heard "turisti" and "Americanos" and cries of housewifely dismay. And we ran and ran and bounced down those steps and back at last to the main street. Then we sauntered and the panic left us and we put ourselves in her place. In the front porch; Joan thought of Ballyduggan and me of Cardiff and, goodness, we knew how she felt, and then we giggled and we couldn't stop until the sight of two policemen at the city gate sobered us.

"Committing a nuisance they call it. They'd have us in jail."

"Think of the headlines. Ballyduggan Barrister flies to Jailed Wife. Cardiff Consultant refuses to comment. Two women claiming to the British tourists arrested in Yugoslavia on charges of committing a nuisance. Yugoslav authorities hint at further, more serious charges. Is MI5 involved?"

"Will you be good enough to smile at those two peelers and say something to them."

"You smile and I'll say goodnight. Don't make an invitation of it now." And dignified as two English ladies we bowed to the peelers and wished them goodnight and they saluted and we hailed a taxi and went home.

We didn't address one word to the driver apart from the name of our hotel. We'd learned that lesson.

And quietly in the back seat she wormed off her pants. "I'm soaked. Hadn't a minute to finish. I'm bloody sure I'm not going to ruin my good black sitting in those."

"Sure, I'll put them under the seat. Somebody'll be glad of them. They're a good pair."

And so we got back and to bed and I lay in my bed and said, "Look at me, drunk as a lord, smelling of scent, naked as a whore and happy. What's happened to me, at all? I'm even talking like you."

"Great. Now go you off to sleep and let me say my prayers."

"Prayers? Why? You never said them before."

"I never saw two peelers here before. I'm saying me prayers."

CHAPTER 7

In the hangover mornings I would remember my lost clothes and sometimes quite passionately long for them and wonder if I'd ever see them again and whether I could claim compensation for them. But while I had Margaret's things and Joan's tea-coloured dress, pressed and neatly altered by the little chamber-maid, I was somehow able to suspend my worries. I visited Franko regularly, but that was now becoming a social visit, part of the pattern of our mornings.

I was damn grateful to Margaret and we asked the Boyds out to dinner to show a little appreciation. We booked a table at a private enterprise restaurant Franko had recommended to us and met them first at their usual pub.

When we joined them they were sitting at a table with a little, old sad man in a ginger tweed jacket whom they introduced as the Professor. Too old to work, too old to re-adjust, he was an anachronism in Yugoslavia, his academic dignity long since drowned in the drinks he had cadged, his erudition now only a kind of turn put on to ingratiate, to impress, like a memory man in a music hall. He spoke all the European languages except the Celtic ones, but mouthed them all through toothless gums and with a tongue too thick and gross to be controlled now by the wet, senile, thick lips. Pale blue eyes that questioned the harsh world like a baby's punished it knows not why, and all the time the fat, puffed face pleasing, ingratiating, frightened. An old-fashioned liberal in the sixties when left, right, east, west, right, wrong mean no more than the beat that soldiers march to. Left, right. Left, right. Left, right, but it must be left or right, one or the other. A hard time for your old-style liberal, for whom life had seemed so clearly rational, so manifestly only a matter of weighing the reasons and seeing the light. The Professor was old, redundant and irrelevant in our world of opportunistic solutions, driven out of his cloister, forced to fraternise, on the fringe, with the poor whom he had earlier regarded from an objective distance that was fit.

Poor Professor. Poor ignorant scholar.

He had been promised an introduction to us because we represented the Celtic world which he had as yet, as yet, mark you, not mastered. As yet, and he was seventy-nine. Joan hadn't the Irish and he was too old for beauty so I was the "pièce de resistance". He wanted to hear the sound of Welsh, the noise of it, and I said some poetry to him. But what he wanted to hear was something in Welsh that he knew in all his other languages, his Greek, his Russian, his French, his German, his Turkish, his Rumanian. Obviously, I must say the Lord's Prayer. And, of course, trust me, out of practice, I forgot the words after the first twenty or so, and the others, all good Catholics, were listening. But I passed it off and shoved in a bit of modern poetry and who was to know, there in a pub in Yugoslavia, despite those ancestral nonconformist ghosts that raised their palsied fingers and cried shame. You never get away, do you? I never can remember what goes on in Welsh after "on earth as it is in Heaven". I have a block on "Give us this day our daily bread", I wonder why. Early socialist indoctrination probably. But to go and shove in a bit of irrelevant poetry in the middle to tide me over the hump, that was blasphemy. And blasphemy is a real sin, whether you believe in the other or not. Blasphemy is bad manners, indifference, insensitivity, intolerance.

It was inhuman to get up and leave the Professor there alone in the pub to go and have a meal in a posh restaurant. But a senile memory man is a bore, you have other obligations besides the ones that tear your guts with pity. You have a duty to be gay, you can't impose your sentimentalities on other people, you have to move on, leave, abandon and then live with yourself.

I called for another round to give us the strength to turn our backs on him and to give him an excuse to stay on there after we had gone. Drink was rapidly becoming my answer to every moral problem, why did it have to be so cheap, so easy? I had lost a hell of a lot more than my clothes; a different landscape, a different wardrobe, scent, booze, new people, and I was like a bobbing little boat that trails its anchor and that any wind could blow whenever it listed – like that almond tree "whose tender leaves do tremble everyone in every little breeze that under heaven is blown".

But the weight of my anchor was still there and I felt its tug when I looked back to wave goodbye to the Professor and saw his loneliness, his symbolic isolation in that pub, in that world; his innocence which was his crime. He sat, an old, small, fat man, surrounded by the empty glasses of other, passing people, nursing the dregs of his own drink to make it last just a little longer to postpone whatever it was that waited.

Traitor, I put him out of my mind. Old Wordsworth knew his onions all right, "strength attends us, if but once we have been strong". But the strength of weakness is much more powerful, if but once we have been weak. If I'd asked him to join us for dinner nothing would have happened, he would have discouraged people, put them off, would have been, in his senility, his scholarship, armour plating against the events of that night which were the beginnings of my real fall from grace. You get what you give. I paid for my sins against the Professor.

It was an excellent meal and Alan Boyd and I talked British politics which is my favourite thing and I'd been missing political gossip and comment and the shared vocabulary of politics, and Alan Boyd provided it all and I was so happy and quite free of the constraint I'd felt in their apartment. Joan had this strong politics phobia; fair enough, I suppose, in someone from Northern Ireland, where, I gathered from her, it's considered ruder to ask a man how he votes than to ask if he keeps a mistress. She talked with Margaret about something else. I've forgotten what, if I ever knew. They were sitting together across the table from Alan and me, with their backs to a party of Americans who were loud and boisterous. I didn't see how it started but soon they were talking and laughing away with the Americans. It was a typical tourist situation, the superficially extrovert Americans, calling for brandies for us and insisting on welcoming us into their circle, warm, friendly Americans in love with the world, as long as it was prepared to be their oyster. In a while the chairs were shuffled around, English voices took over the restaurant, new bits of conversation began; I was made to speak in Welsh again and got carried away by a lovely bit of cynghanedd and I realised I'd gone on too long and there's nothing, but nothing, more boring than a meaningless music of words.

I fell small and silent after that and sat back watching the six men. The two youngest ones looked thirtyish and had that perpetual-adolescence look of crew-cut puppyish puzzlement so many male Americans wear. One was obviously Jewish, the other as Nordic as they come, and yet both had these physical traits which were unmistakably American. Negroes have it as well. It's compounded of good food, arrogance, strong teeth, money, brashness, sentimentality and plenty of hair. All six of them had splendid teeth or bridgeworks, not even my eagle eye was quite sure, and I remembered the Professor's empty gums. Teeth, the symbol of success?

One of the older ones was remarkably handsome, well over six feet tall with a broad but elegant body, long disdainful hands, thick greying hair and almost stridently deep blue eyes. He looked like a successful modern poet and there was a repose about him that seemed to lift him above the hurly-burly. Perhaps he had a very good analyst or had a deep

religious conviction. Anyway, he looked unusually distinguished and spoke very little. By the process of natural selec-
tion he had chosen in the reshuffle to sit beside Joan and he
watched her as she chattered away, with almost scientific
detachment, very Henry James.

I found myself with a very bouncing sort of person beside
me. A dog-person, restless, brown-eyed, lots of stiff coarse
hair like a coconut mat and short stubby fingers in which he
held a tooth-pick which he gnawed and ravished with his
strong square teeth. He was dressed in a blue-and-white
striped jersey, white linen slacks and sandals, but you felt
clothes didn't really belong to him, didn't merge into him, he
was like a dog or a monkey dressed up in a circus. A quick
peep under his chair verified what I'd expected from his face
– horrid, untidy, bare feet with down-curved toe-nails, very
doggy. He was a great one for affection, arms around the
shoulders, tremendous shouts of appreciation, arms raised in
extravagant delight. His name was Toby.

On my other side was a dim sort of man. A stereotyped
American again, tall, well-fed, well-dressed, well-mannered,
so typical that he seemed only a kind of ghost, a shadow of
someone else. I hardly noticed him at first, dismissed him as
dull, he didn't seem to get any of my nuances of speech,
didn't respond to my kind of talk, but then I noticed that he
was systematically breaking in half every one of the tooth-
picks left on the table by the gnawing Toby. Picking them out
of their container one by one and snapping them – so – finish,
and reaching for another one; I wondered if something was
troubling him, which was a crazy thought in that rich, flamboyant holiday group.

I took another look at him. His skin was coarse, not coarse
in patches where he might have had acne, nor coarse from
old boils or chicken pox, but coarse throughout, like a dog's
skin would be if you shaved off the fur. Could you say wire-
haired skin? That's what it was like, anyway, like a

wire-haired terrier under its fur. The sun hadn't affected his colour at all, he was the colour of dry yeast, off-cream with a touch of grey.

Behind his big, smart glasses his eyes were unsure, perhaps apprehensive, as if he was afraid he had cancer and was too scared to go and make sure. When, occasionally he did utter, he did something to his facial muscles – he seemed to tighten all the muscles in his face forward towards his nose, which gave him a clipped, chipped sort of look of intense concentration as if he was labouring with a great thought. But he never gave birth to more than the current platitude. The only interesting thing about him was his Christian name, Birkenhead. Fancy calling a baby Birkenhead when he's already got Pringle for a surname, no wonder he had that hunted look.

Alan Boyd was talking to the last man in the group, a big man in his late fifties, running to fat. His big face was red from the sun and his nose peeling, a big amused face, tolerant and kindly-looking. I felt rather drawn to him but I was cut off by the litter of bottles and a bunch of dahlias and by my efforts to amuse Dog Toby and Birkenhead, both of whom claimed my Welsh accent was real cute. I'd got over my poetic embarrassment and was living up to the frilly black dress and my French scent, being madly gay and frivolous – me the old non-adjuster, old take-it-or-leave-it.

I was putting on a kind of Gwyn Thomas *tour de force* and talking about Wales as if it really bore some relation to *How Green was my Valley*, a book they thought much of. Toby was proudly proclaiming that he'd got a Welsh grandmother. I found this surprisingly endearing because, let's face it, over here Welsh ancestors are carefully swept under the mat if they can possibly be held down long enough. Poor old disgraceful Welsh.

The Americans wanted to move on to a little place they knew where there was dancing. They had paid their bill but I had still to settle ours, Joan being the way she was about currency. They all got up and they trailed out, noisy, dominant, overpowering, rich, leaving the restaurant quiet for the little people.

Poor Birkenhead had been hemmed to the wall by me so, naturally enough, he waited with me while I paid, got my change, tipped and was bowed out. As we stepped through the doorway on to the dark street a flamboyant man came up to me, took my hand and kissed it and made a low bow.

"Ah, madam," he said with a stage-struck foreign accent, "you 'ave enjoyed yourself at my so 'umble restaurant? You will come again, no?"

"It was fine," I said, "splendid. But don't you take that for approval of private enterprise, mind. I'm still a good socialist." And I staggered a bit in the fresh air on drunken, tight, high heels. I wasn't too sure socialist had come out sounding quite right either.

There was no comment from Birkenhead, he just stood there, waiting, and again I thought he was just like a shadow of somebody, just a male shape, but he was a man, which was better than no man.

"Madam is not Americano, no?" the flamboyant figure murmured and came close up to me, his slack, fat belly almost touching me. When he was that close I couldn't but see his tie – the tie of Aberdeen University. I have a relative there and I know that tie all too well. I looked at his face again and it was no more Yugoslav than mine.

"Fraud," I said, "you're from Aberdeen."

"Och, aye," he confessed and switched on an equally stage-struck Scotch, "but you're the first who's twigged me the night," and with a respectful salute he slipped back into the shadows of the next house.

How mad can you get? Honestly, what a way to spend a holiday, but it was lovely to know the granite had such enchanting fissures in it.

My stocks soared with Birkenhead. It seemed to him
utterly marvellous to have spotted the man as an Aberdonian;
I didn't tell him about the tie and when you haven't the looks,
any sort of build-up is a comfort. Not that I wanted to
impress him, *qua* him, mind you, but he was a kind of repre-
sentative of the world of men, if only a shadowy one.

By now the others were away out of sight, but I wasn't
concerned because, as I said, it's a very small city. We'd
catch up.

"I suppose you know where they've gone?"

"Sure, sure, there's no rush. Take it easy."

Take it easy and me in those heels on cobblestones and
feeling the booze a bit. What choice had I but to take it easy?
I was picking my way like an old rheumaticky hen on a
muddy run and terrified of falling flat in Margaret's good
black dress.

"You in a hurry to join them?"

"Not particularly," I said, to be polite, "only Joan and I
have to go home together, our hotel is way outside the city."

"O.K. We'll pick them up, but what about showing me a
piece of the place first, I'm just one of your dumb
Americans."

"All right. But on one condition. Can I take my shoes off?
My feet are killing me."

"If you want polio or hook-worm, sister, it's your funeral.
Go right ahead."

"Oh, thank God for that. It's better than taking off your
corsets, honest."

"Jees, you say the cutest things. Just go on talking, can't
you?" and then, of course, I couldn't think of a thing to say
so I upped my skirts and ran. Ran, mind you, pretending to
be skittish and seventeen, with a tall lumbering American
having to run after me. I don't know why I ran, your guess is
as good as mine. Didn't run far though, believe me, with the
fags I smoke I can hardly blow out a candle, breaks Mike's

heart. But it's no good screaming carcinoma at you till they can name the substitute for fags, because fags are substitute for so many other things, if you see what I mean.

But at the end of my Olympic run we were within sight of the old pier and the great guardian fortress, dazzling, white as Christmas in the floodlights, and I could talk about that. I'd read the guide book.

"But there are so many things you must see. How long have you been here?"

"Two days only."

"Don't you love it here? The Boyds are hoping to settle, you know. But I'm surprised at you Americans coming behind the Iron Curtain, giving your good American dollars to the commies. Won't they have you up for un-American activities?"

"We just stopped off for a coupla' days. This is business. We move on to Italy to pick up a few ideas."

"What sort of business?"

"Gadgets."

"That's about as useful as saying 'notions'. What d'you mean, gadgets?"

"Well, sister, it's this way. Affluent society. Right?"

"Right."

"So what happens when this guy has everything, but everything? You kinda have to give him a gimmick, gadget, like you said, notion, see? Take a peek at this liddle beaut," and he took out of his pocket an object made of harsh chromium and thick black wire. It was folded flat on to itself and he opened it out with loving concentration. Eight right-angled black legs attached to a sad sort of empty round and then, from underneath, flick, a black head with eyes. A spider's head. *Ych y fi!* Of course, he wasn't to know how I feel about spiders.

"See," he said "you put your glass, an Old-Fashioned, in the circle, set the mechanism, like so and your drink comes over to you, across the table." And he set the obscene thing moving, crawling on the white marble wall of the ancient port. I was nearly sick.

"Pretty, hmm? One of the Italian bright boys dreamed that up. That's gonna go great." I never in life saw anything so indecent, so vulgar, and he watched it with such love, it was like a mother revealing her child's deformities. Horrible. I looked up into his face, in case this was meant to be a macabre joke, but, no, his face was serious, intent, with that clipped, chipped look on it, wound up as if to strike twelve.

"Yeah, it sure is gonna go great. Make any party."

God.

He put his arm around me as he watched his toy and I looked over the sea towards the island where I'd written my love letter to Mike and with a stab of guilt remembered I'd still not posted it. Must do it tomorrow, tie a knot in my hankie. But I didn't have a hankie, only a tissue. I don't suppose people often go around tying knots in tissues; Birkenhead certainly looked a little surprised, but I told him it was an old Druidic custom, to keep spiders away, and he bought that.

The mechanism in the horrid toy wound itself out and before he could wind it up again, I turned to move away.

"Where is this place they've gone to? Joan will be wondering what's happened to me. Let's go, shall we?"

"Yeah, yeah, it's right here, on the dock side, where the music is."

"Wait till I put my shoes on, then. Oh, the agony. What with mosquito bites and the heat, let me tell you. First degree murder."

In the café, bar, dance-hall, what have you, we found only the two younger men at a table with a magnum of champagne in an ice bucket. Bottles, yes, in my time I've been moderately intimate with bottles of champagne – but a magnum, that was something else, that was really something. I touched it reverently before sitting down to ask about Joan and the others.

"They took a dander round the city. She says you should make your own way back, if they miss you again and if you're kinda occupied. Harry's shooting a heavy line on Mrs Miniver."

"Mrs Miniver? Who's Mrs Miniver?"

"Joan, the lady, the peach, for Godsakes. Ain't she little ole Mrs Miniver for real?"

I couldn't, then, remember who Mrs Miniver was, but they all seemed to agree, so I accepted it, along with a glass of lovely, lovely bubbly. Actually it wasn't all that lovely, very local I'm afraid, but the idea of it was lovely, the pretty beaded bubbles that tickled my nose and the magnum and the ice bucket and the napkin. It went straight down to my toes and I could feel the torture soothing out of them. My shoes were already off. After a second glass one of the young ones asked me to dance and dance I did, barefoot. Don't ask me what we talked about, I wouldn't know. "Do you come here often," I expect, but we laughed a lot and I wasn't too puffed at the end, thank God.

Back at the table they'd got a new magnum and two more females. For the sake of my morale, heaven be praised, they were only two English spinsters, definitely middle-aged and markedly spreading, at least 42 hip. Mine are 38 incidentally. When I saw the hips of them and the slight gentle down along their cheeks I felt, momentarily superior to them, middle-aged, I thought, and spreading. Me – menopausal and all! But on the spur of the spot you never realise you're old, do you? I keep catching myself thinking my contemporaries are ageing; and then, remembering that I'm there too is like changing gear too late on a steep hill. But at least I'm not spreading and I was barefoot and there was that little old gold band on my finger. Oh, I'm nasty. I made no attempt to enjoy Flo and Sue and their talk of medicine in Sheffield, which they went on about because somebody said Mike was a doctor. I don't know how they came to be at the table nor where eventually they went. Unless Birkenhead – what a name – was trying to prove that he could pick up girls when my back was turned. They sort of drifted into my consciousness with the clarity you get for long moments when you're tiddly and drifted out meaninglessly after my third glass.

It was when I was dancing with Birkenhead that the realisation hit me that I had a kind of relationship with him. It was entirely accidental that he should have been the one to wait with me at the restaurant. He hadn't chosen it, and I certainly hadn't, wouldn't have, chosen him and now there we were, in a sense partnered off in "that jig each lout and slattern knows". He had by way of a claim on me. He was, incidentally, a damn good dancer or the champagne was telling me lies. He was tall and strong and held me firmly and I'm telling you I needed some holding. The kids have taught me to do their modern dance things for fun and I really went to town on that dance floor. Wouldn't have dared in Wales, of course, not in public, professional dignity and all that old crap. What the young in one another's arms must have thought of my exhibition, I honestly shudder to think.

There was one big moment of clarity in my haze on the dance floor. Birkenhead was holding me firmly, strongly and very malefully and he whispered in my ear, "You know something, Innes, you know something? I want to gore you."

"Good heavens. Do you? Why?" He didn't answer that, but swung me away from him and executed a pretty turn opposite the band. Fair enough, it was a damn stupid question, did I want the moon too? But "gore". Horrible word. American vocabulary can be so insensitively vulgar.

Then he hugged me again and said, "Well, how's about it, sister?" I felt it was an awfully cold-blooded way to go about a seduction. He could hardly have expected me to say "yes" just like that, could he? I mean, I'm not used to these modern ways. But, mind you, I didn't say no. I only said "Let's go and join the others, shall we?"

But the others had gone, Flo and Sue and the young men, only the end of the champagne was there, the ice all melting, the napkin sopping and sad. We sat down again and squeezed the last drops out of the bottle.

"Well," he said, his face pinched, the eyes behind the smart glasses still fearful, if slightly glazed, "do we go to my hotel?"

And I couldn't; it wasn't virtue, I won't pretend; it was just his bad, bald technique. I couldn't take it like that, straight and unvarnished.

"It's getting very late. Some other time."

"Aw, kid, come on, don't tease."

"I'm not teasing, honest I'm not. Joan will be wondering about me. Truly. And this is Margaret's dress. I couldn't in her dress. D'you know what I mean at all? Take me home now, there's a good boy."

So, hand in mature hand, we walked back through the silent city where they were washing the streets and it was more like Venice than ever. We got a cab at the city gates and I was impressed by his good manners when he got in with me to see me safely home. I should have known better. As soon as the taxi moved off he took off his glasses, put his arms around me and started to kiss me. He had a real way with him, and remember, I was full of champagne. I found myself responding like a flower turning to the sun – and the sun was Birkenhead, God help me. Things got to a pretty pass; I think the euphemism they use today is "petting". My mind was a kind of kaleidoscope, one second thinking of the driver and the angle of his mirror, then forgetting and getting carried away by the things he did to me, then coming back with a gush of guilt, thinking these lips on me, these hands, they're virtually anonymous, faceless; a stranger I don't even like very much. Another kiss and mindless again.

It was straight sex, like a farmyard, animal semi-coupling, like kids. But if it had to be, perhaps it was better that way, there was no emotional disloyalty. There was no emotion; this was just playing around, Kinsey Report peeping translated into a little actual secret experience. Put it down to scientific curiosity, a bit of active pornography, if you like. But it was certainly one up on the Kinsey Report.

Fortunately a swish of guilt coincided with the driver's slowing down for the hotel and I was able to come down to earth before he stopped. Birkenhead came up to the door with me, smoothing his hair and replacing his glasses, and he reminded me of my promise to go to the Casino with him the following night. Maybe Mrs Miniver would join us. And off he went into the dark and I went into the bright hotel foyer, my eyes dazzled by the lights, my make-up eaten off, my hair trolloping around my face, and I thought the night porter couldn't fail to see what I'd been up to. I was scared of seeing Joan, those shrewd blue eyes would recognise all my symptoms. She'd have my life.

Quasimodo slithered up to me as I was about to dash past the reception desk and held out our key to me.

"Madam?" I asked, "Signora in camera?"

"Non, signora."

Coo, where was she? I looked at the clock, nine minutes past three, oh Ballyduggan and Reverend Mother, what was she up to? I took the chance to tidy myself in the ladies in the foyer before she saw me. My face in the mirror was heaving back and fore at me and my eyes were stark and I was drunk as two owls and the colour of an electric light bulb, white and obsolescent. No, obsolescent wasn't the word I was looking for – but a word like that, kind of shiny and transparent, translucent? No, incandescent perhaps. Oh, to hell. Where could she be?

I straightened my back to go out again but I was unhappy about hanging about in the foyer because of old Quasimodo.

Silent seduction I could not cope with, not again. But if I left, she'd have to cope with him; then I remembered Harry and the distinguished, poetic look of him. He'd bring her right up to the hotel and see she was safe, so I risked it. I was already washed and combed and killing off mosquitoes with a towel when she arrived a few minutes later.

She looked happy and alight, but without a trace of guilt about her.

"Where the hell have you been, duchess?"

"Och, he's such a nice wee man that one, you know that? But he's away tomorrow. The only half decent one of that bunch. And what were you up to, at all?"

"I got landed with the one called Birkenhead, with the glasses. And we drank champagne and we danced and he brought me home in a taxi. And were you a good girl, Mrs Maguire?"

"Cross my heart and hope to die. We only talked. I told him about the kids and Ballyduggan and he told me about America. They're all stinking rich, by the way, especially thon old feller. What's this you call him? Clay, yes that one."

I went on slapping mosquitoes on the wall and she sat straight on the edge of a hard wooden chair, looking fulfilled and satisfied. But it had nothing to do with sex, she had an aura of virtue. I think she got more pleasure out of talk, what she called "good crack", than out of anything, and I wondered, not for the first time, if she wasn't perhaps a little frigid.

"They've invited us to the Casino tomorrow night. Will you come?"

"No, not without Harry. You go on ahead. I'll see the Boyds, I promised we'd be round. And were you a good girl, Innes Gibson? Can I see something in your eye?"

"Only champagne, dearie, only champagne. I necked a bit in the taxi, nothing to speak of. Just enough to pass myself. I've never been to a Casino."

"I'm sorry he's away. He's in business and he likes music. We could have gone to a concert and he wouldn't go to sleep on my hands, like some. I've invited him to Ballyduggan anytime he's across the water."

"He's not a poet after all, then? I have never in life, I promise you, met a duller man than that Birkenhead Pringle. He isn't a person at all, I wonder what goes on in his mind. I suspect he only responds to stimuli, like plants. Stand beside a girl in a nice place and you put your arm around her. Take her to a dance place and you order champagne." I only just stopped myself from saying dance with the girl and tell her you want to gore her. The duchess wouldn't then have let me go to the Casino, so, half-honest, I said, "Get into a taxi and you take your glasses off to kiss the girl. All conditioned responses. I promise you, I can't remember one thing he said." I was, of course, remembering one, but not telling. "I have to work so hard to keep a conversation going, I let him kiss me for a rest."

We went to bed that night in long-sleeved blouses and stockings and wrapped the sheets around us like shrouds to discourage the mosquitoes. We tied headscarves down to our eyes and sprinkled our pillows with camphorated. The stink was powerful so we scented handkerchiefs and tied them over our faces like crooks, only two pairs of eyes peeping out. We would have terrified anything less intrepid than mosquitoes.

CHAPTER 8

Outside the hotel the next morning, waiting hangovered, hangdog in a thin drizzle for a tourist coach to take us somewhere. We'd forgotten where, for the minute, but we'd remembered, almost too late, that we'd bought these tickets for Sunday and this was Sunday.

A thin rain, sea-side rain, not wetting, penetrating, but standing out on our woolly cardigans and on our hair and eyelashes, light, gentle, too light to do more than land on us and stay perched. A queue from the hotel; orderly English, Yorkshire voices, London, middle-aged, decent folk, the women in dresses and cardigans and cellophane hoods, bright red sunburn, mostly plastic teeth, the men hearty and talkative, repeating jokes. And there was Ernie, Ruskin College, W.E.A. who'd been everywhere before, instructive and solemn, believing in learning, indifferent to anything aesthetic, in slack grey pants that looked inherited, scratching at his crotch as he prepared our minds for whatever it was.

We stood waiting, indifferent, idly scratching our own bites, silent, and when the bus came we got seats at the back and went to sleep again. A rocky, jerking, public sleep, punctuated by the courier's voice and short stabs of wakefulness when the landscape seemed so unreal as to be part of the dream. Sudden small pomegranate trees on the roadside, the fruit like little quick flames; bright, bright fig trees and water melons in village plots. Women going to mass in their local costumes and the courier explaining the significance of their caps, which indicated their marital status or ambitions. After thirty you wore a different cap if you were still unmarried. I woke to think that very sad and slept again.

A barren mountain landscape. Great hunks of rock embracing small cultivated patches, olive trees, goats, donkeys, gipsys and still that gentle rain. A long journey.

And by lunch-time we were in Mostar, a Turkish town with a famous single-arched bridge and mosques and Mohammedans. A violent place, of nineteenth century history, a place that gave a local habitation and a name to Macedonian massacres, Bulgarian atrocities and Serbian assassinations. In the market place the people had a wildness about them, an untamed look. I thought of Franko and his justification of infidelity, "I am Bosnian boy". Here that affirmation made good sense. And I now saw the poor slashed wrists as his first pathetic assay upon our brave new world. If you can't live like them, you can at least try to die like them.

A gipsy woman with brown bare breasts and nipples like ripe damsons was feeding her baby at the roadside by the market. All around her was market refuse, rotten fruit, bits of wood, cardboard, melon skins, dung, and she sat there oblivious, dignified, Madonna. Our crocodile march was halted while cameras clicked at her. She looked up, saw what they were doing, and tore the baby from her breast to rest screaming its protest across her knees. With both breasts bare she shouted her fury across the street and pelted the cameramen with all the refuse within range around her. She never took her eyes off that crowd, her abuse streamed out and the tomatoes and melon rinds and dung came soaring through the air, never missing a mark. It was splendid and dignified and right. Such a proper response to those scrubbed Americans, those respectable British, those sociological Germans. I felt quite restored by her.

Herded, we went to a Mohammedan house, took off our shoes and sat uncomfortably low on cushions. The parrot-courier told his tale and we put on bright, interested faces. They gave us rose-water to drink and it was pink and sickly sweet, like drinking cheap scent, the sultans can keep it for me. I wish I knew the answer to tourism. That house was a genuine Turkish house, a mediaeval house and should have been wildly interesting, but with everything on show, ordered, organised, it was quite destroyed. Even the old family pieces looked bogus and bought. Laid on.

After that it was a Turkish restaurant and we woke up properly to marvellous food and the local wine, with the famous bridge on the label. We shared a table with an Italian called Umberto and his secretary. He was a funny man and told us a stream of dirty jokes, mostly about priests. A performing person who made you wonder what it could be like when he was alone without any sort of audience, did he fade like the Cheshire cat or was he like the tree in the quad, not there if you weren't looking? The secretary was English and there was a good school behind her, and not too far behind, either.

After lunch we went to look at the mosques from which earlier we had heard the wild unearthly gramophone record of the muezzin's voice calling the faithful. We were out of our hangovers by then and appreciative. That strange wild place said something to me about political history. I'm not sure what it was, but it was something comforting about the permanence of real people, about their kind of rock quality over which armies and ideologies sweep, topple, break and fall away. I had a romantic conviction about those people, that place, that was entirely irrational, completely at variance with my normal welfare-state political responses. I see it now as a sentimentality, but I am none the less committed to it, more pragmatic, more open to doubt, matured by a bare-breasted gipsy woman and men with wild dark eyes.

It was good to be travelling back along the same route, to be able to enjoy the countryside without the courier's intrusions. He'd done all that on the way in and his voice was tired now. Even W.E.A. Ernie was at last subdued. We halted for a comfort stop about halfway home at a roadside farmhouse where they had a sort of open-ended shed stocked with wine and beer bottles. Under a fig tree on the patch of grass before the farmhouse a group of local men sat at a table, their faces were like the Old Testament and they had a dignity and dominance that was as humbling as the look on Byzantine mosaics and icons. The calm of them, the arrogance, the personal assurance, pinpointed the aggressive insignificance of our world. They made me feel all woman, slavish, abject. If one of those had murmured "cinque minuti" I would have felt so deeply honoured, but to them we were as nothing, not even the duchess got a second glance.

Umberto, the Italian, bought drinks for us that we drank under a second fig tree and as we stood there, laughing at his irreverences, a fig fell with a rich, ripe smack at my feet, bursting its skin and showing its purple heart. I picked it up and buried my teeth in it and it was warm with sunshine and tasting of honey and tobacco and ripeness. Umberto turned to the men at the table, with a gesture towards the tree, and one man spoke and said "Take. God's gift."

The Italian left for a branch and swung himself up into the heart of the tree, filling his pockets and the front of his blue and white striped jersey and promising to bring us a feast. But I couldn't wait for him, couldn't be denied. How often in life is one given a fig tree to climb, figs to gather? I couldn't wait. I got a chair for the first hard bit and, clumsy as a carthorse, I pulled myself up into the lovely airy greenness. It was like being inside a poem, like a folk song. The big ungraceful leaves flat, like half-formed hands, green figs like small goats' udders; rounded, delicious handful; the swing of the whippy branch beneath me, the exquisite threat of falling, and Umberto singing as he moved and jockeyed for a better foothold.

I was young and green and clean and the sun was warm and my green isolation was like a kiss, like warm water, like yellow daffodils.

I looked down out of my green sky and Joan was watching me, her face turned up, waiting and open with laughter, and I knew that this was my holiday. I threw a fig at her and she caught it and laughed aloud and then I rained figs on her, pelting her, teasing her like a small boy, till she had to cower from me and cover her head with her arms. I'd never before understood about Lesbianism, but there in the tree, I felt the pull of it momentarily. She had looked so beautiful, so fitting, I was forced, pushed to respond, to answer, she turned me into a small boy. I was eight and cheeky with it.

And then they tooted from the bus and it was time to go and we left that lovely place, the men still sitting idle under their tree, the small boys tidying up the refuse left by the turisti and the woman of the place counting up her dinars.

The clouds came up again with the approach of dark and the rain was shrouding the city like net curtains as we came upon it from the mountains.

It turned colder with the rain and I reverted to my own red suede suit to go to the Casino. I didn't give a thought to its suitability for Casinos. I'd never been to one, fair play, so I couldn't really imagine it. But, on the other hand, I'd seen casinos in the movies and I'd read James Bond. I honestly believe my first basic thought was the middle-aged one of keeping warm, but what the old gonads were really up to underneath I couldn't swear to. Did I revert to my own clothes because I wanted to revert to my normal self to stand on dry land again, or was it because my valid and accepted excuse for putting off Birkenhead the night before had been Margaret's dress? Were my own clothes a defence or an invitation? I promise you I didn't give it a thought at the time, but you don't need to think when those old instincts take over. Honestly, we are pretty helpless, aren't we, when you think of it, such a prey, I mean, and most of the time we don't even realise it. But other people realise, that's the rub. Gives me the creeps, honest. Slips of the tongue and all that – good heavens, once you begin thinking how you give yourself away you feel paralysed. And so often the you that you give away is a complete stranger. It's worse for me than for most, with all those psychiatrists that Mike knows and I'm so compulsive. Talk about calling your soul your own, what hope have you, when the old psyche keeps bursting out bright and green as a pruned rose bush to tell the truths?

Birkenhead called for us with a taxi but Joan was adamant in her refusal to join us for the evening. We could take her to the Boyds' apartment and they would see her safely home. But we must go, she and I had been together too much, a wee break would do us both good. I wasn't a bit reluctant to accept this, there was probably something in it, and I was dying to go to the Casino. Not because I wanted to gamble, that's not one of my things at all, but I wanted to see it, watch it, wanted it like going to the theatre, naïve as a child for the circus.

"Now have a good time," Joan said, as she left us to run through the rain to the Boyds' door, then she turned again to add, "and don't forget, Innes, that our money's going like snow off a ditch."

The approach to the Casino was very grand as far as I could see in the rain and the dark. We went skittering down a broad flight of steps with the shapes of palm trees and cedars beside them. Pale statues, dimly elegant, caught in the wet with their pants off, great plops of sound from fish ponds and fountains, white balustrades and balusters, and then a man with a golf umbrella under the discreet light above the Casino door.

But inside it wasn't at first very Casino Royale, there was a kind of long hall-stand for coats and a fat man at a desk changing money for chips. But only foreign currency. You couldn't gamble with dinar, which was after all only logical. I had only Yugoslav money because my English fivers had gone on fags and whisky and my illegitimate others were distributed in various bits of my luggage – lost. But Birkenhead, that perfect American gent, staked me, anyway. He bought me ten white chips, and as he collected them, along with his own, a man sidled up to me and said, from the side of his mouth as if he'd practised in a looking-glass, "Say, is there another way out, sister?"

"Search me," I said, "I only just got here."

"I must find some other way out." He waved a sheaf of dollars at me, very like the White Rabbit waving his paws and whiskers.

"Ask the bloke with the umbrella," I suggested and he gave me such a look of hatred, you'd think I'd turned a gun on him or spat in his eye.

"Bitch," he snarled at me, and pitched out into the wet without his hat or his overcoat. I never found out who he was running from, his wife perhaps, or his creditors, or maybe "umbrella man" was a code word and he might have thought I was the black haired, black hearted lady agent. But he set the tone of the evening for me, created my "suspension of disbelief" as they say, began the crazy mood that cut away all that dry land I may, or may not, have been trying to build up around my feet with that suede suit.

When Birkenhead and I went on into the actual gaming room I realised the suit couldn't have been more wrong. There were only about five women there, all dressed as though for a coronation, brocade and Balmain, silver and sequins, and me in wet red suede and you know how it marks in the rain. Poor Birkenhead, and he was so pathetically conventional; well, he had to be, didn't he, I mean, shadows by definition conform. All I could do was live up to the look of me and I stood in the door and said, much too loudly, "Coo, I've never been to a casino before, tell me what to do, Birk." There happened to be a pause in the play at that moment, winnings were being distributed and the croupiers being tipped, so everybody looked up at my voice and I had, by accident, said the rightest, best thing. There was a mutter of "virgine" and one woman said "Follow the virgin". I was the virgin and a virgin is apparently as highly recommended by practised gamblers as by practised seducers. They made way for me and gave me a chair at this long table covered with lines and numbers, as intelligible to me as an astrological chart, and with this roulette wheel at the end of it. I sat down, terrified.

The croupier encouraged us to place our bets and they all waited and watched me. All I could think of was "think of a number, double it, take away what you first thought of." I can't tell you how awful it was. And all those faces and the clothes.

To comfort myself I thought about Mike and put five of my chips on the date of our wedding and on red because of the suit. Actually that was the nearest number, it wasn't really a matter of choice. The women, being more credulous than the men, followed my example but did something else, very complicated, on the side, that I'd need a computer to work out. But the thing is that I won. I won a great pile of pink and white chips and I nearly died. I blushed like a thirteen-year-old girl and the blush became a menopausal flush and my hands shook, palsied, as I collected the chips the croupier pushed towards me with this stick thing he had.

The woman who'd said "Follow the virgin", and had made room for me beside her, won a packet too, even bigger than mine. She was a very pretty, thirtyish American, delightful and charming to me. She whispered that I should tip the croupier for my winnings and offered to explain what she had done with this fancy side thing of hers, but I had to say "No thank you, I'd never understand. Just leave me with these numbers, I'm a terrible dunce."

But dunce or not, I'm not a complete nit and I could still hear Joan's last warning ringing in my ears, "Our money's going like snow off a ditch." It was so unlike her, so out of character, that it had hit me and I decided there and then to be quite firm with myself. I put all those good pink chips, that were worth five of the others, into my handbag and resolved to play only with my white ones and to play only as long as my white ones lasted. My bag was a big, solid, cream leather one, bit enough for passports, guide-book, air-tickets and the usual trimmings, and Mike's letter, still waiting to be posted. What I must have looked like, hoarding away my pinkies into the bag and closing it with a positive click, in that smart, rich set complete with umbrella man, I shudder to recall, but at least I made a change for them.

I didn't win on the children's birthdays, nor mine, nor Mike's, and my white chips were down to three. Then I thought of the number of years Mike is older than me and plunged my three and sneaked one, only one, pinkie from my bag and I won again. I put back the one I'd sneaked from the bag and kept playing again till I was down to two pink ones. I look at them hard, thought of the English fags they'd buy, picked them up and they joined the others in the bag.

I'd been chattering to the nice American girl who had very charitably said my suit was a nice colour and I'd told her about my luggage and how I'd spend my winnings on some new pants and a bra, especially in view of the rain which made it impossible to wash and dry things overnight. We got a bit crazy and giggly together and she insisted on calling my bag my pants till we compromised on shirt, which was a bit more fitting. After the final click of my handbag Birkenhead, who hadn't won a bean, invited us to have a drink at the bar they had in a room beyond where the table was. This was a very classy room with big soft white-brocaded armchairs on a dark grey carpet, pale grey wallpaper and lights in sconces. There were some quite horrid bits of ceramics, late nineteenth century Czechoslovakian, I should think, with that nasty high gloss and slavish adherence to realistic detail.

Celia, the American girl, and I made rude remarks in Italian about Birkenhead and ordered the very best imported brandy, that he had to pay for. I was ashamed that she saw me with Birkenhead, it was unfair to me, to Mike, but I guess he was ashamed of me too, I was just too odd, so we were quits, I suppose.

We sipped our brandies in the white armchairs and talked about Europe and politics and America and she was a liberal and a violent about Viet Nam, and Birkenhead was silent. He went away to get more brandy when she began on Civil Rights and then more people joined us and it was a party and then she and I went together to the ladies' place. You're probably thinking that I suffer from lavatorial complex, the way I'm always in the ladies. Perhaps I do, but I've always found lavatories very significant places. For a start, you can lock the world out and retreat in there and there's only you, pared down, basic. There's rarely any distracting clutter about the place, only you and the pan and a window you can rarely see out of. Temporarily a "room of one's own", a cell, a coffin, a true place. You could hardly lie to a flush of water.

Celia and I had each other's life histories by now, she was married to a rich man, but had been brought up poor – Italian immigrant parents too honest and too simple to integrate. She'd had to take her mother shopping when she was only as high as the basket on her mother's arm, and the scars of condescension and ridicule got on 103rd Street, New York, were like second degree burns. She revelled in her American dollars, her American man, it's nice to be tender when it's legal like this. She was on a sentimental journey to grandparents in Siena while her man went on making more lovely legal tender in Philadelphia, here I come. Yugoslavia, Iron Country, she'd visited to thumb her nose, defying the dollars.

My stupid bag was so big you could never find anything in it. I always have to tip it upside down to paint my face. My pinkies came pouring out with all the other paraphernalia, lovely, pink, plastic clinks, rolling and running and laughing at me; the colour of cyclamens, the promise of pants. I ran them through my fingers, kissed them, bit them to make sure they were good, but I never counted them, that would have been sordid, they were so pretty, so smooth, so clinky.

"Celia, I'm going to keep one or two of these for souvenirs. They'll amuse Mike and the kids. After all, look how many I've got. Isn't it marvellous? And all thanks to old Birkenhead Pringle, God help him. Better go back to him, I suppose; he's carrying his cross tonight, all right. Misery acquaints a man with strange bed-fellows."

I'd planned to go back and sit in my same white chair but when I set eyes on it I reared back like a frightened carthorse. I said it was white brocade, didn't I, with this sort of tangled fringe thing around the bottom and outlining the arms? God, if you'd seen what my moulty red suit had done to that chair. It was a pink chair now and the rough tangle of the fringes had been working overtime, like steel-wool or a wire brush. Should I sit in it again and try to hide it or move far away and pretend it wasn't me? I hadn't the guts even to tell Celia, she'd go and do something about it, she was like that. But I'm a coward. All I wanted to do was run. I stood in front of it, but it was much bigger than me. How the hell I'd covered so much of it, I just can't tell, unless it was when I was wriggling a bit before we went to the lav. The waiter was coming up to wipe the table beside me and with a gay grimace I said something, God knows what, to keep his attention on me and off that chair. I was tacking about the chair, manoeuvring myself between him and it, like a Labrador with fleas. Suede, you may recall, is stiff stuff, it doesn't drape the human frame, and as I humped around, dog-like, the tail of my skirts swished a glass off the table and it smashed and that gave the waiter something to do, thank God.

Birkenhead was watching me with agony and horror in his apprehensive eyes. I think it was the only expression I ever caught him directing at me, I didn't think he could take much more.

"Feel like moving along?" he asked, dying to ditch me.

"Yes," I said, "shall we stagger?"

Birkenhead went to tip the waiter for the trouble I'd given him – he didn't know half of it yet – and I said goodnight to Celia who said she'd see me tomorrow at Birkenhead's cocktail party. It was the first I'd heard of the party but I wanted to see her again and was all delighted and said "Great". I wasn't quick enough to see whether Birkenhead's face registered another expression at this, but when I did look he was taking it like a man.

They cashed my pink chips at the pay desk, which was just like those they have on fairgrounds outside the Fat Lady and the Giant Rat, kind of timeless and contemporary. I insisted on dollar bills, single ones, even though they took longer to count, and I was keeping a sentinel eye on the door in case the waiter saw that damn chair. But I wanted to have a pile of money, money that looked like something. I'd won 81,000 dinar. You can work that back into pounds for yourself; it sounds so wonderful in dinar, I'm keeping it that way. It made a pretty enough pile in dollar bills, too, let me tell you, for the likes of you and me anyway. And I owed it all to Birkenhead.

I felt badly about him. I was obviously not his cup of tea and to have been in the wrong clothes was probably, for his conventional soul, the very end. And the zany, unsophisticated line I'd shot, to match, must have been a hell of a trial. I wonder how he'd explained me away; wife of a client, maybe, or a possible designer of his obscene gimmicks? He must have offered some explanation, he couldn't possibly have confessed to inviting me from choice.

The money and my disloyalty at the Casino made me take his arm on the way out and press it closely to my side.

"Thank you very much, Birkenhead, I have enjoyed myself and I'm sorry I embarrassed you."

"Think nothing of it," he said. Really, he might at least have said not at all; perfect gent, no manners.

"No, honestly, I know how you felt and I am sorry. And thank you again. Now I have some money, I'll buy myself some new pants tomorrow."

"And you'll let me see them, of course."

Easy, Innes, easy now.

I laughed that one off and said, "Come on, let's run for it. This bloody rain."

There were dozens of those broad slippery white steps with the rain spanking off them and when we got to the top I was puffing and blowing with all the weight of my forty odd. Birkenhead turned masterful at the top and took me almost brutally by the arm to guide me to his hotel which was next door to the Casino. The rain was pouring down and I could-n't stand arguing there, not to a man whose hair was plas-tered to his head and hanging over his brow in a monkish fringe above his streaming glasses. So in I went, into this very posh hotel, very new and rich, with rubber plants and pages whenever you turned to look and the smells and sounds of arrogance and wealth, and English the dominant language. Birkenhead was his usual silent self and I was busy taking it all in, to report back to the duchess. There were other people in the lift as we went upstairs so nothing specif-ic was said about the reason for my visit. Was I sheltering from the rain, coming in for a drink or what? I didn't really like to ask. There had been last night and the taxi, but there'd been the Casino since then. No, it was all right, he'd lost interest. That about showing him my new pants was just a conventional Birkenhead response, penny in the slot stuff.

He put his key in the lock of his door but it wouldn't open. "Damn" he muttered and hammered on the door and then came noises from inside and a cross, sleepy voice came, a doggy snarl, "For Chrissakes I'm coming. Shut up, can't you?" and the dog person, Toby, was there, dressed in nothing at all and God knows not expecting visitors. Well, hardly, like that. He grumbled and swore at Birkenhead in his houndstooth voice, but said nothing to me at all, not a word. He turned away from the door and pulled on a pair of tartan underpants with long legs, down to his knees and slack in the behind.

It isn't every day of my life that I'm greeted by naked men and my savoir faire quite deserted me. I turned to go away, but Birkenhead pushed me into the room, with scant enough ceremony. It wasn't really a room they had, but a sort of suite. There was a great big L-shaped room with three beds in it and the other end furnished like a sitting-room with couches, coffee tables, desks and arm chairs. Great big windows opening on to a balcony running the whole length of the room.

I saw a black bathroom near the door, with three wash-basins, like the Three Bears, so I excused myself and went in there to let them fight it out together. I did what I could to my hair and powdered my nose again and shuddered at the sight of my pretty white blouse, all out in spots. In spite of the initial shock of it, I'd been reassured by Toby's doggy pres-ence, there was no risk now while we had an audience, so I went cheerfully out of the bathroom thinking that I'd soon be home, showing Joan my winnings. I'd get them to order a taxi for me.

Toby was still sulking in his tartan trews and scratching in the hairs on his chest, but the temper in the room seemed to have died down and they'd obviously come to some compro-mise arrangement. And compromise is the word indeed, now that I come to think of it.

Birkenhead shepherded me out on to the balcony where there were wrought-iron tables and chairs, and said "Pour us some drinks while I sort this out, will you, kid? Scotch for me."

There were glasses out there and lots of bottles and some melty iced water in a jug so I poured him a stiff Johnnie Walker on Mike's theory that whisky makes men impotent and I poured one for myself for company. I moved away to the far end of the balcony away from the angry voices, which were raised again now. But it was nice to be alone out there watching the storm and the sea that was breaking in, white and beautiful right up to the walls of the hotel. It was a roofed-in balcony, of course, I wasn't out in the rain.

Birkenhead called out, "Be with you in a minute. Got a little something to attend to," and I didn't bother to answer or look around. The storm was more interesting; I heard various shufflings and thumpings going on behind me, but I didn't bother, I thought, if indeed I thought at all, that they were moving the beds around because of their quarrel and didn't want to sleep near each other any more. Then Birkenhead came up behind me with his drink, put his arm around me and turned my face up to kiss me. What's a kiss for 81,000 dinar? We took a few more sips, interspersed with a few more kisses, and then he said, "Let's go sit down." No harm in that, I thought, but there was, oh my word, there was, because he'd carried his mattress out on to the balcony while my back was turned and that's where he sat, pulling me down after him.

The curtains were drawn across the windows of the room and there was no sign of Toby.

"Whatever happened to Toby?"

"Oh well, he kinda left us."

"In his tartan trews?" I asked, horrified.

Birkenhead didn't specify. He had a great gift of just not answering, had that bloke. He said so little, anyway, that you were never surprised when he stayed mum and you let things slide when you never should have done, like then.

I was holding my glass of whisky between us like a crusader's sword but he took it out of my hand and laid it on the floor, and then he laid me, on the mattress. There was a certain inevitability about it, it was almost good manners on my part, sort of doing the right social thing at last. I don't even have the excuse that I was drunk, I knew what I was doing, and fair play to Birkenhead Pringle, I enjoyed it. He was good. Probably learned it from a book, but he really knew how. I never once thought about Mike, I was utterly selfish, being pleasured as they used so honestly to say in the eighteenth century.

I had a fit of silent giggles when it was over and he was lying spent and heavy in my arms, because I'd been complaining to Joan that he was only a ghost person, an automaton. Now I wondered whether I ought to write a paper for some learned society concerned with E.S.P., to say that I'd made the acid test and had been laid by a ghost. I know I was in my own clothes then – God, didn't I know it? – you should have seen the state of his sheets after mollocking me around in that red suit – so I couldn't claim that it was the loss of luggage that turned me wanton that night, with never an ancestral voice shouting "Thou shalt not". No, it wasn't drink and it wasn't the clothes, but it was partly the way-out things I'd been doing – climbing fig trees, wearing scent, winning money. You are what you do, after all. Do unaccustomed things and you get unaccustomed compulsions. It was like you get a different view of the world from the back of a horse. And there I was, swept to bed by figs like udders, and sunshine and lolly and gratitude and politeness, toujours la politesse. And since it looked as if it had to be somebody, I thanked God it was Birkenhead, because really he was such a husk, it hardly counted. Not so very different from masturbation, only less personally degrading, and I was also satisfying my scientific curiosity, wasn't I? No need now to die wondering whether different men, different ways.

The really odd thing though was that I felt no guilt at all. I carry a load of vague guilts around at home that drive me to depression and the family up the wall, and here I was now, with plenty to have a real wallow about, as cheerful and elated as a bride, perky as a winter bird, pleased and pleasured.

Unfortunately, Birkenhead fell asleep with all his weight on top of me and I had a wicked struggle to wake him up and then we couldn't find his glasses in the tangle of bed clothes, but we made it in the end and I set off for my favourite haunt, the bathroom, quietly delighted at the chance of a bath for free.

Poking out of the bathroom door, however, were a pair of feet, I'd know them anywhere with those down-curving nails like claws. Toby had by no means "kinda left us," he'd merely removed his mattress to the bathroom floor and was snoring there. Thank God he was asleep at least. I don't think dogs go in for voyeurism. But I needed that bathroom: well, I mean who wouldn't, after all those shenanigans. I didn't dare wake him again, he might bite me, and I was damned if I'd wash with him there, so there was nothing for it, I'd have to go as I was, like a whore who does it in the park or on sand-dunes.

He took me back to our hotel in a taxi, through all the rain. Some of the streets were flooded with thick sand-coloured water and the little boats were rocking and bumping in the harbour as though possessed. It was stimulating and exciting after all the sunshine: melodramatic rain, like symphony music, not like the quiet, absorbed, inevitable, dreary rain we know in Wales; I liked it, wanted to walk naked in it, wanted the beat of it on my skin. I turned to tell Birkenhead how it pleased me, but he'd gone to sleep again in the corner of the taxi. I couldn't be bothered to wake him up, not again, so I left him without a word of thanks or a Goodnight and told the driver to return him to his hotel, like any load of old rubbish.

Joan was asleep, shrouded and masked against the mosquitoes, when I got back, but I wasn't having any of that.

"Wake up, duchess, come on, wake up. Look what I've got. Look, 81,000 dinar. Lots of lovely lolly," and I threw the whole bundle of notes all over her as she struggled to sit up in her bed. Green dollar bills, floating about her head, settling on the winding sheet, falling neglected on the floor and me dancing a jig like an Irish tinker around the room.

"Jesus," she groaned, sodden with sleep, "are you telling me you won all that money? Are you sure you came by it honest?"

"Well, yes, more or less. I won it in the Casino but Birkenhead had to stake me, so I owed him something, if you see what I mean."

"Innes Gibson, you didn't–?"

"Well, yes, I did and what's more, I enjoyed it. Now don't start on me, duchess. Keep it for tomorrow."

"But with yon fellow? Sure, you don't even like him. And take all this bloody money off me. Go on, gather it up. I'll not touch it. Wages of sin, that's what it is."

"Come off it, Reverend Mother. It's because I don't like him that it doesn't matter. There's no conflict of loyalty and all that jazz. It's quite simple, like having a good meal." I was kneeling beside her, collecting my dough while it was still safe.

"A good meal in the pig's trough?"

"Balls, duchess. You've got to be able to divorce sex from love. Who have I harmed tonight, tell me that. I've paid my debts. I'd rather be solvent than chaste."

"You don't have to talk like a whore, never mind carrying on like one."

"Oh, come on now, fair play. It's not whorish to be realistic about sex for once. I mean, you can think of sex as a gesture of friendship, a kind deed, a Christian act, if you like. Anyway, a social service."

"Chuck it now, Innes, chuck it. Don't say any more. Stop it, stop it, stop it."

"O.K., O.K. we'll talk about it in the morning. I'll just get washed and get to bed. Sorry you're not pleased about my winnings."

"We will not talk about it in the morning. I won't hear another word about it."

"Lord, I'll have to wash my pants and where the devil will I put them to dry, in this rain?"

"Put them on the back of your own chair – not near mine, mind you, and let me go back to sleep, you whore. You haven't left any of that money round me, have you? Couldn't touch it, it's like cobwebs."

"Prig."

She humped her back on me and slept.

CHAPTER 9

She woke me next morning just by staring at me. I could feel her eyes through the dregs of my dreams.

"How the hell you can sleep like that; innocent as a baby; and all you've on your conscience."

"Duchess, I've nothing on my conscience. Sorry, old dear, there's no sackcloth and ashes. Sackcloth and ashes when I'm all restored and happy and my purse is full of dollars? No duchess, no conscience. I enjoyed it and I think he did and nobody's been harmed."

"But your man, woman dear, your poor Mike."

"He's not in it. Anyway, jealousy's not smart any more."

"Will you tell him?"

"Are you mad?"

"I wish I could think of you going to confession at least."

"But you can only confess to guilt. No guilt, no problem."

"But that Birkenhead fellow, sure isn't there a problem of taste – well, I mean, if you want to say it was like a good feed, well you'd want to eat it off nice plates and with silver cutlery. Yon fellow's like an enamel dog-dish that's been left lying and a tin spoon."

"Yes, you've got a point there, I'll admit. But who else was there and last night he made it so impersonal, so uncommitting, you weren't involved with him, only with it. He's irrelevant, he doesn't count, so Mike's not affected. There's no other man in it, he's only a kind of cipher – as if I sat on one of your phallic symbols. Can you see me perched on a spouting?"

"Christ, that's you. Make me laugh. Oh well, sooner you live with it than me."

"I met ever such a nice woman last night. You'll love her. An American. In the Casino. She had a Balmain dress on.

You'll meet her tonight."

"Where?"

"Birkenhead is giving a cocktail party in his hotel and she's coming."

"Well I'm not, for a start."

"Oh, don't be stuffy, love, it's just a cocktail party – there'll be no shenanigans there."

"Are you telling me you can face that lot again after last night? He'll have told them, you know that, don't you?"

"You know, I don't think he will tell them. He won't boast about conquering me. You, yes, he'd put it in the papers, but he's probably asking himself this very moment how he ever came to do it to me. I can just see him, can't you, sort of shaking his head and rubbing his face to remove the memory. I'm so much not the kind you show off about. Back in America he may boast about the bird from Wales, he'll have me a sort of female Dylan Thomas by then and jazz it all up, but not to those people, not to the ones who've seen me. He has to have classifications, categories, and I don't fit any of them. He'll work one out for me, eventually, but not yet. Unless they do it for him, of course."

"He'll tell them, even if he tells them he did it out of charity. I don't trust yon man, I tell you straight."

"But you'll come to the party, won't you?"

"No, I'm for the Boyds' again."

"But I promised Celia I'd come and want you to meet her."

"Well, you go and take a drink to pass yourself and fix up to meet her tomorrow on your own."

"All right, then, I'll do that. And I'll wear Margaret's dress again. That'll keep me pure. What'll we do with the money I won? How shall we celebrate?"

"We won't. I'm having nothing to do with it."

"Oh, you are a bore, duchess, honestly."

"O.K. so I'm a bore. You'll have to put up with me. I'm a

bore and you're a whore and we make a pretty pair. Now move and pass me the camphorated."

It was the worst organised cocktail party I've ever attended. Perhaps Birkenhead had forgotten about it till his guests began to arrive, it certainly had that sort of ad hoc feel about it. For a start, he didn't have bottles about the place to fill people's glasses. Every time anybody wanted a drink he'd ring a bell marked room-service and wait till a harassed chamber-maid or waiter, who was obviously busy with something else, appeared and he'd order each drink from them in a hectoring, over-loud voice.

I can't think why this was. There'd been bottles about last night, but perhaps he had delusions of grandeur and wanted service at his party, like hiring help in bibs and tuckers for big events in American homes.

He wanted bits and bobs for us to nibble, olives and crisps and stuff, but he couldn't make himself understood and they brought up a plate of chips – hot ones – and a plate of green salad containing a few olives. He was the host and insisted on doing everything himself and he got mad with the tired waiter, which the waiter didn't like, and his face got more and more clipped, the eyes more and more apprehensive and he didn't speak to us at all.

All his friends from the restaurant were there, except for Joan's Harry, and there was another pale young man called MacPherson who was a secretary to the older man, but no Celia. Celia was obviously to have been the *pièce de résistance* of the party and in between the business of the waiters, he kept telephoning her hotel to try and remind her. I think he'd used the promise of Celia to make the others come. They certainly wouldn't have come for Flo and Sue and he had had me.

The others were polite to me, if uninterested, but Birkenhead himself scarcely looked at me; I might as well have been an old tin can. I must say I expected a bit more than that; I mean, after all, he was my first deviation to the primrose path, and in spite of what I'd said to Joan, he was in that sense special. You don't sleep with – and on – somebody you can't quite place. But that's what he gave me, I promise you. I won't deny that I was a bit piqued. But I chattered away, party manners, and was much nicer to Sue and Flo than I'd been at the champagne place. I even recommended a good doctor for Flo's mother's arthritis and listened to a digest of Sue's latest Reader's Digest. We sat, three old trouts, drinking our gins and wondering what the hell we were doing there.

Toby was in a huddle with the younger men, they looked like conspirators, like business men, like old gossips. Birkenhead, when he had the time, circled them like a rogue elephant, wanting in, suspicious, distracted, pulled stupid by the demands of hospitality and his ill-concealed hostility to the closed-in, tight knot of his friends. Clay, the older one, the one reported to be stinking rich, stood about, looking bored and leafing through a pile of advertisements for guided tours. Irritated by Birkenhead's compulsive carry-on with the telephone, he threw the brochures down and, touching Birkenhead lightly on the arm, he offered to take over the telephoning for him. The phone was on a bedside table far inside the L of this large room and Clay sat on the bed, cut off from the party, twiddling the dial and yelling for Celia's hotel about twice in every five minutes. I could just see his feet from where I sat with my two buddies.

Birkenhead and Toby vanished somewhere and the chips were cold and congealed, but somebody had absent-mindedly eaten the salad.

Flo and Sue discussed the relative merits of Sheffield shops and nobody joined us.

I died to go, but felt I must wait till Birkenhead reappeared – my morals might have gone to hell, but I still remembered my manners. Of course, if he was a ghost he might never materialise again. That was a thought. But before I could voice it, there was a shattering crash from the bathroom and Toby erupted through the door and shouted, "This is the end. I'm through," and he leapt like a police dog across the room and out of the door into the corridor, snarling "The damn bastard, the damn effing bastard." We three tried to pretend we hadn't noticed anything, Sue and Flo had to pretend they hadn't heard that word. Then Birkenhead came out of the bathroom, his face white and a great red mark across his brow and a white welt rising in the middle of it. And this was supposed to be a party.

Birkenhead also left the room.

The conversation with Sue and Flo flagged. I decided to leave and was on my feet when Clay called out, "Innes, come here a minute, near me?"

He was lying on the bed now and had given up bellowing down the telephone. It was almost dark in there with only one low-watt light bulb burning beside the telephone. Clay took my hand and pulled me down to sit on the bed beside him.

"Kid, I'm lonely in here. Talk, can't you."

"My God, what a party. Birkenhead has walked out on us. What the hell's wrong with everybody? I get invited to a party – I only came in order to see Celia and she can't be found – I'm left to talk to those two trouts, I'm ignored by my host who has a free fight in the bathroom and then departs without a word. And, incidentally, I've had one, small, warm drink."

"Oh sure, well, skip it. Just a little business problem. Think nothing of it."

All this conversation was conducted in whispers because of the semi-dark, I suppose, and then suddenly, out of the black, as it were, Clay called out: "Mac, get in here, boy." I nearly jumped out of my dress at his bellow, it was like a sudden hand on the shoulder when you think you're alone, and the Macpherson one came shambling up to Clay's bed with a glass in his hand. He was a pale young man. Tall and thin, his head pushed forward, an assistant's stoop. His hair was thin too and worried-looking, thread-bare, but I liked his face. He looked serious, concerned. In spite of his name there was a kind of Jewish warmth and tolerance about him. This he may have caught from Clay who looked as tolerant as Santa Claus, a secular Friar Tuck.

"Get them out of here, boy, get them out and lay on some goddam liquor in here for Chrissake."

"Yeah, Clay, O.K., coming up."

"Don't get anything for me, please, Clay. I must go."

"Oh, baby, no. Baby, you stay and talk to old Clay, poor old Clay. I just wanna talk to you. You're kinda cute, kid." He did look rather lonely and pathetic there, fat and ageing, his big face flushed and peeling with sunburn.

"No, really, I must go." I put down my now long-empty glass beside the telephone which he had abandoned but he held my hand and wouldn't let me go. He had a grip like Fate or death.

"No, don't do this to me baby. I wanna hear you talk is all. Just one little drink with old Clay." I was standing beside him as he lay on his bed, that grip still viced on my wrist.

"No, I don't suspect you of having designs, my dear Clay, it's just that I have to go. And if Birkenhead comes back it'll be ridiculously embarrassing for him."

"The hell with Birkenhead. He's moving on. Forget that creep. He's not for you, baby. Come on, siddown, siddown." Macpherson succeeded somehow in indicating to the other guests that the party was over, there were departing noises from the other end of the room. I tried to pull away, thinking of Flo and Sue; I seemed to be making a habit of losing those two. He held my arm and he was strong, strong as a furniture remover, I really had no choice. Also I did want a drink and

Clay was the only one of them I'd ever really wanted to talk to anyway. And he was reputed to be a millionaire. You don't meet all that number of millionaires in a lifetime, after all; in a way he was like that fig tree. One shouldn't pass up experiences.

So I sat me down on the edge of his bed and he put his heavy, remover's arm around my waist, but there were no shenanigans, his hand moved neither above nor below the belt. It was a friendly, gentlemanly, courtly gesture; supporting me, holding me on, like two kids on one swing.

He disarmed me completely (I'm sorry about that pun, it was accidental) by talking about Wales. It's so odd how one responds to talk about one's native land; nationalism, patriotism if you like, ought to be such an anachronism and yet it's still one of the most dominant sentimentalities. I mean, look at the Chinese, for a start. I'm a complete sucker on Wales.

Clay said, "How come you still speak in Welsh? I got the notion the British suppressed all those old Celtic lingos."

"The British, my dear Clay, always do what is, to coin a phrase, politically expedient. Elizabeth First wanted to establish the Protestant faith, so she had the Bible translated into marvellous Welsh to wean us away from Catholicism. Terribly important that was. Later on, especially in the nineteenth century, it seemed politically expedient to suppress the language. You must surely know about the infamous Royal Commission that enquired into the state of religion and morals in Wales in 1847?"

"I'm just a poor dumb American, baby, you tell me."

So I told him. On fire with ancient wrongs and happy to talk, I told him what the wicked Commission had said about my people, quoting the choice bits we'd learned at school, bits like "The Welsh language panders to prevarication. It is a manifest barrier to moral progress." Clay loved those and clapped his hands and growled deep belly laughs, especially over "Welsh country women are universally unchaste".

When Macpherson came back with bottles and ice and fresh glasses on a tray, Clay and I were cosily *en rapport*. I was beginning to feel hungry but didn't like to mention it, what worried me was that I'd start rumbling, which wouldn't be pretty at such close quarters. Macpherson poured the drinks and then he, too, sat down at the foot of the bed. Down there in the shadows it was hard to see him properly, but he was companionable and nicely uncompromising, if you see what I mean.

It was a nice time. The conditions as far as I was concerned were almost ideal. This isn't disloyalty to Mike and my kids. They were out of this. I was on my own now and successfully on my own. Here were two men amused by my chatter, enjoying me as a person, the lights were nice and dim and my self-consciousness was all away, the drink was good, the conversation excellent, though that assessment may of course have been the drink. Clay and Macpherson seemed to me sound on American politics and properly perturbed. They were both virtually illiterates as far as book-reading went, but that was fine for me, another feather. I was getting to be very hungry but I hadn't rumbled yet and I comforted myself with the thought that they'd probably give me a good dinner. So I sang for my supper and filled up meanwhile with gin and tonic.

But something happens in time with gin, doesn't it? Something happens to all sorts of things with gin, in fact, bladder, ovaries, what have you, but to time most of all. When, finally, I had to announce that I was killed with hunger and must, really must go, if only to eat, they were wildly apologetic. We sorted ourselves out to go down to the restaurant and I got a chance to powder my nose.

You know how I feel about bathrooms and I promise you there's nowhere like one of those for telling you how drunk you are. When you sit, perched, in solitude, alone with yourself, then you can measure just how far you've moved away from yourself. If you don't know yourself on the lavatory pan, you never will, and when you have to close your eyes because the brush in the corner is beginning to heave at you, then, sister, you know something. And all those mirrors where your eyes are staring at you with a manic light behind them and you're not a bit worried and you giggle and make monkey faces at the accusation, then you better watch out, you really had.

I wasn't really very long in the bathroom, but the temptation of all that water for free went and got the better of me and I took a quick bath. The lovely hot water overcame even my hunger and the towels were fluffy and vast. I had to put on a new face as well, of course, but even with that it shouldn't have been after ten o'clock when we got down to the restaurant. But it was.

Clay and I got to the restaurant doors alone. Macpherson had gone somewhere, I assumed that he just wasn't hungry, but he said he'd be back and I'd drunkenly promised not to leave without saying goodbye to him. It was just one of those promises though.

The restaurant was closed and dark against us, the service over, the waiters gone. I was as disappointed as a baby denied its bottle and just as cross.

"Take it easy, take it easy," Clay counselled me, big as a bear. "Say, why don't we just go back upstairs and get the goddam room-service to send up some sandwiches, I guess anyplace else would be closed."

"Listen, don't talk to me about room-service. Look at those chips they brought. Lord, I could even eat those now, cold as they are. Oh well, there's nothing else for it, I suppose, but for heaven's sake let's hurry or room-service will be over too."

So back we went and they brought us these quite horrid sandwiches with raw onion in them and a coarse kind of salami and no butter on the thick bread. Very nasty; but I do admit it was our own fault and if I'd been doing room-service there after Birkenhead's party I think I'd have added a soupçon of strychnine to the raw onion.

There was still no sign of Birkenhead but I suddenly remembered him.

"Whatever happened to Birkenhead Pringle, Clay?"

"I told you he wasn't for you, baby. I told you."

"You didn't have to, love, you didn't have to, but what was the fight about, anyway? It's as good a way as any to break up a party, I grant you, but why?"

"Business, just business. Just a question of who has the goddam cash and Toby boy has it there. Pringle is out on his threadbare arse."

I felt a twinge of sympathy for my old friend Birkenhead and then I remembered how he'd walked out on me, ditched me indeed, come to think of it, and how he'd looked at me like an old tin can. I wondered what would happen now to his horrid old gimmick that was to have made any party go. Any party but his own, God help him.

When we got back to the room it seemed only natural to go and sit on the bed where we'd been before. It didn't occur to me to sit anywhere else, we'd sort of warmed that place, you know how it is, and the only light burning in that big room then was the little one by Clay's bed and we kind of gravitated.

We sat there and the sandwiches were very nasty, but I had to eat something or die; Clay took one look and shook his head and sat like a Buddha watching me wolf, King Cophetua and an ageing beggarmaid. I didn't wolf long. God, they were awful, but Clay had ordered champagne with them so I had to make do with that.

We were lying there quietly, companionably on the bed, sipping our champagne, when we heard a key turned in the lock. Clay whispered to me to hush and switched off our little light. "Take no notice," he said "and they may go away." I thought this terribly funny at the time, can't think why. And Macpherson's voice came and a girl's. The girl was laughing and sounded young but we couldn't hear what they said and we lay quite still and silent. I saw Macpherson's hand click on another bedside light, a little dim one, like ours, beside the bed in the long leg of the L. They seemed to be laughing a lot and I heard drinks poured. Clay whispered, "Just lie low, baby, lie low. They'll go. They'll go." I was lying with my head on his pillow and his arm was under my neck, his other hand playing with my fingers.

We lay on, just waiting for them to go, easy, not wanting to be bothered.

But they didn't go. My goodness me, no, on the contrary, and they had no intention of going for at least twenty minutes, for they suddenly appeared, starkers, both of them, and made for the bed. It was a very big room, remember, as long as a cricket pitch at least, with these three beds in it, and Clay's was right away in the far corner of the short leg of the L. With our light off they couldn't have seen us. When my incredulous Cardiff eyes lighted on those naked bodies I struggled to get up and away but Clay had been cleverer than me. The arm under my head came up and his hand closed on my mouth and his other hand closed on my fingers and held my hands like a manacle. What would you have done, what would anyone full of drink have done? Again Clay whispered, "Take it easy, baby, take it easy, don't embarrass them. They'll never know. Just close your goddam eyes."

But you can't close your ears as well and I must confess I took a furtive peep. The scene was all Matthew Smith. The curtains across the balcony thrown open to the starlight, the small light off now and these great, sculptured curves rearing and convoluting, white carved granite, Laocoon, John Donne, the beast with two backs. Clay's grip on me was easing now – now that I could do nothing; well could I? It was by then just a case of if rape is inevitable, lie back and enjoy it. But I didn't enjoy it. I was crying like a baby. Crying for them and for me and scared even to sniff. Then Clay took my hand and held it in his crotch against a little thing, not much bigger than a thimble, a little firm thimble and heaved and jerked under my hand and then it was over for him. And I felt sorry for him and kissed him, my ginny tears embracing him as well now as we lay imprisoned there in silence. But my tears changed, the way they can with gin, to threatened giggles as I started to write a short story in my head about Clay. About the millionaire business man, I called him Plasticine in my story because I needed the alliteration and it kept the malleable connotation, and, after all, Americans seem to be called almost anything. "Plasticine's problem was his penis. It was minute." I thought that would get them. Good punch line to kick in. But suddenly it was over for the others too and I heard Macpherson grunt "So" and he got up and slapped the girl's bottom and showed her the bathroom. And she said, "*Was gut,* no?"

"Great," said Macpherson, "great; now get going, sister, get going."

Still Clay and I lay on. I was afraid to move a muscle and dying for a fag, and Macpherson was getting dressed again and I thought it couldn't be much longer and he'd never need to know, poor boy. But, would you believe it, as jaunty as a robin Macpherson came padding through the semi-dark up to Clay's bed and in a harsh and bitter voice, kept low and forced, he said "That'll be twenty dollars, boss. I'm damned if I pay *and* provide the entertainment."

I felt exactly as if I'd been hit hard, on the nose. I fell on my nose once when I was little and that was exactly the same sensation, one of incredible bewilderment at the sheer pain, the very centre of your being all badgered and broken and a giddiness with it that seemed to lift you up and out of the actual situation. I think I was in a genuine state of shock.

These were nice people. I'd liked them both and yet
they'd allowed this terrible thing to happen to me. They'd
used me in their voyeurism, worked it out, planned it. I
wanted to be sick but the girl was in the bathroom and if I
vomited into the ice bucket she'd hear me and then she'd
know too. I had to save her at least, poor little toad. I eased
my retchings with the dregs of champagne. And then I was in
a towering rage, crying and defiled and covered with
cobwebs and all in whispers and Macpherson demanding his
twenty dollars and me still sitting on that bed. Clay bestirred
himself and put on our light and felt for his wallet and leafed
through it, but all he had – millionaire – were hundred dollar
bills. He looked stupidly up at Macpherson, "See," he said,
"all big ones goddam it."

"You want I ask a tart for change, boss?"

"Hell, boy, you should have thought of this one."

I was moaning in my pent-up fury, rocking to and fro in
my distress, and then from somewhere I remembered the
dollar bills in my bag on the floor beside me. I reached down
for it but my hands were shaking too much to open it and I
pushed it at Macpherson, "You knew we were here, didn't
you? You knew it all the time. You laid it on for Clay."

"I've laid on a good many things for Clay, sister. Lay
being the operative word."

"There are some dollars in that bag. Take what you want
and go away for God's sake before the poor little girl finds
out about us. For God's sake go, can't you? I can't take much
more of this."

"O.K. O.K. Take it easy. Thanks, kid."

And then they went and I stood up and that grip again on
my wrist and that peeling Santa Claus face looking at me and
begging for something, forgiveness perhaps. And I slapped it
with all my anger, but the grip didn't relax. He turned his
face away, looked down, away from me.

When he spoke his voice was slow and slurred, heavy

with drink, inarticulate. "Listen, you gotta listen. You gotta learn somethin'. Discrimination you talked about, right? Toleration you said, and sympathy, right?" His face still turned away from me and the fringe of sparse grey hair along the back of his neck pathetic and defenceless. "But, baby, not only for niggers and yids and commies. Not only politics, kid, politics and race. Christ, those are only what you see. Them, why they even had goddam banners.

"Look, you wouldn't persecute queers, right? Not you, baby, not you. Make a minority and they've got you, glued, Miss Lonelyhearts. But, Jesus, don't you begin to understand? That's all I'm asking. Toleration. I have a problem. Don't I rate a little help?" He was feeling for words like a blind man, through a fog of alcohol.

"But Clay, why me, why involve me? You liked me, we got on, we were even happy. And now I feel – oh I can't tell you, I'm numb. Sick and numb. And drunk and shamed. Why did you so shame me?"

"Don't cry like that, baby, don't. Chrissakes, don't. One thing, there wasn't no involvement, don't kid yourself. Then, you were sorta like an instrument. Innes, nice Innes, was irrelevant, see? God, why do I have to be stoned? Tell me how the hell I say this; don't want to be crass, kid, but any whore would have done. But you I kinda liked. Like you were a friend, kid, like cleaner, right? And you ain't no kid, you been around."

"I'm sorry, Clay, I'm sorry. But I can't take it. Failure of sympathy, O.K., but our resources are limited, you can't spread sympathy thin like syrup and I'm too full to understand or want to try. All I want is to go home. Let me go home, Clay, let me go home." And the tears still streaming and Clay's box of tissues going down.

"No, you don't go yet. First we get this straight. Listen, now don't get wild again, but you and Pringle last night, that was different because he's straight? Me you like, him you don't, and just because he doesn't have his little tricks it's better? With a guy you know is a rotten four-flusher?"

"I didn't really know that. I've only your word for it even now."

"You take my word for it, sister, believe you me."

"He told you about me, then?"

"Yeah, told us all and I mean all. He's that kinda guy. You sleep around, you, with a John Bircher and it's fine. O.K., but me, I don't even rate a little sympathy. I'm the goddam guy with problems, remember?"

"What was that you said about Pringle? You're not telling me he's one of those John Birch racists?"

"One of them, nothing. Sure he helps run the organisation."

"Oh no, oh God, no. Clay, just let me go. I forgive you. It's all right. I just have to go now." And I kissed him where the mark of my slap still showed and wrenched my hand away with the kiss and left him in the wreck of that room.

Macpherson had snapped on the main central lights as he left with the girl, in a gesture of defiance, a kind of bitter comment, and in their harshness the room had a desolation about it like an antique battlefield. Sour with old drink, stale air and sex, bitter with burnt out fag-ends and old indifferences. One fawn curtain, half pulled back and hanging awry, had a leering, furtive, remarking look to it, like one raised eyebrow on a corpse. I wanted to stand there and cry "Help", but who would hear and who would care? It reminded me of the market litter around the gipsy woman in Mostar, the dung, the melon rinds, the squashed fruit, the refuse. And because that's what I'm like, I realised that refuse and refuse are the same word. Refuse is what you refuse to have. I think this little moment of my own kind of thinking was what got me through the drunken, unsteady torment of the hotel corridors, the lift, the brilliant foyer and finally, praise God, the taxi that got me home.

Joan was reading in bed when I came in. I locked the door behind me to keep everything out and then leaned back against it for support.

"Jesus," she cried, "whatever happened to you? You look raped."

"I have been, in a way." She crossed herself and murmured, "Holy Mary, Mother of God preserve us."

"No, don't distress yourself. I'm all right." I collapsed like an old sack on the hard chair beside her bed.

"Do you know what voyeurism means, duchess?"

"Yes, I do."

"Well, I got involved in some of that. I was conned into it."

"With that Birkenhead fellow?"

"No, he'd ditched me by then. No, not him. I understand a bit about the voyeurism now. It isn't that that's really killing me. You'll think I'm mad, but that bloody effing Pringle turns out to have been in the John Birch movement. And – oh God help me – those hands, those hands on me. All my talk. He's irrelevant, I said. He's not a person. I never bothered to find out. Ghost, I said, a mere symbol. A symbol for hate, the negation of everything I believe in." I was crying again and my words came gulping forth, punctuated with great rasping sighs.

"And he's penetrated me – do you realise that? That has been inside me. What have I done to my Mike? Remember that picture of somebody shaking hands with Goering when he was captured? That's me. Oh God, I'm going to be sick."

I made it to the lavatory just in time and Joan followed me, practical as ever, with the air-freshener. When the first, worst retching was over, I lifted my head and she was there tall and beautiful, the ugly feet bare, clutching the aerosol to her chest, frightened, out of her depth.

"Better?"

"Yes, but there's more to come. Don't leave me."

"No."

And then it was finished and I wiped my face. "The wages of sin," I said in a weak croak, "the wages of sin is sick."

"Come away to bed now and sleep it off. Take one of those tranquillisers Mike gave you and you may give one to me too."

"Yes, I will eventually, but there's something I have to do first. I have to do it. I must."

"Och, woman dear, come to your bed. It's late."

"Just let me do this one thing."

"All right. Let's get it over with whatever it is."

What I had to do was have a bonfire. I had to have a ritual, symbolic burning of my pants. It wasn't enough to swish them down the lavatory with the vomit, I had to see them burn; my irrationality wasn't simply drunkenness, it was the atavistic thing about fire, like the beginning of Lent or something.

The only place I could think of, befuddled, to have my fire was in the wash basin in our bedroom. Mad, I know, but I wasn't quite myself and Joan could do nothing with me.

I tore up my guide book, the bills and receipts in my handbag, the brochures about tours of the district, a few remaining picture postcards, and on top of them I put my pale blue nylon pants and one symbolic dollar bill on the top of that. I struck a match and lit the dollar bill first and then the papers. I don't know if you've ever tried to burn a pair of nylon pants. It's not as easy as it sounds. There isn't much of them, God knows, and nylon's supposed to be inflammable, but the problem is that they've used the wrong word, it just doesn't flame, it kind of smoulders and sulks and then curls up into mangled lumps like chewing gum somebody's worked at for a long time.

There wasn't enough paper to keep up the blaze; I went frantic trying to find more bits. Joan refused to let me raid the lavatory, thinking of the morning. I tore the notice about

mealtimes and rates off the door and that made a handy contribution. The smoke and the smell of burning was horrible,
but I turned to my handbag again and there was my letter to
Mike.

"This has got to go too. Can't post that now. Not after
this."

First the envelope, Dr. M.T. Gibson accusing as it blackened and curled and went.

Joan snatched the pages from my hand. "Don't," she said,
"don't do it."

"Must. Go on, put it on."

"Will you not think of him."

"I am. Think too much of him. He's not to have that now."

"Oh," she said, reading the odd line, "he'd give his life for
it, so he would."

"Burn it, duchess, please. Those pants have got to go and
we've nothing else left. There's something about love letters,
anyway. This isn't the first I've burned. I'm always rushing
into print and regretting it. You write at night, say, in a great
gush and the letter arrives with the burned toast in the
morning, all incongruous and pathetic by then. Go on, put on
a bit more, didn't your mother tell you not to read other
people's letters? Yes, you bring yourself to the point of complete emotional nakedness and you write it all and it gets read
between a final notice for the rates and a directive from the
hospital about the provision of bed pans. No, this is wiser,
this way. Shove the rest on."

"What if the postman had read yon letter? You'd never be
sure in Ballyduggan. They'd be reciting it on you at the
wakes."

"And I'll tell you something else, too, duchess. A love
letter is a marvellous gift, but it can be too big a gift from the
likes of me. You dare not, your nasty old self reminds you that
you'll fight again, hate again, shout scorn again, and where
are you then, with all that in black and white as they say?"

"Aye, perhaps you're right. You wouldn't want them all that certain, sure you wouldn't. But it seems a pity."

Writing paper was much more effective than glossy guide paper and at the end of Mike's letter we had the pants reduced to lumps the colour of nothing, that would never go down the waste pipe. But we turned the taps on, nevertheless, and the charred paper came floating up and nothing went down. I plunged my arm in and collected the lumps I could feel in the mish-mash of burned paper but that availed us little until Joan took a wire coat-hanger and straightened that out to clear the plug hole. Thank God she began to laugh then, at the picture of us plumbing in the small hours, and the laughter brought me back to life and now I began to worry about what the chamber-maid would have to say about the state of that wash basin.

We got the water to go down, but it left a crust of charred paper all over the sides and when I'd cleaned that out with tissues, which had of course been far too precious to burn, Yugoslav tissues being what they are, there were great brown scorch marks that quite defeated me. Joan was less concerned about the chamber-maid. "Sweeten her with one of your dollars and say nothing." Unlike me, she doesn't scare easy.

"I'm sorry, duchess, what a holiday I've let you in for."

"Wouldn't have missed it for the world. God knows I'll never forget it. I'll think of this in Ballyduggan in the winter and the kids fighting and crying and I'll not hear them. And sure, wasn't it me that peed in that porch and fell on the steps? When I think who I might have had in your bed yonder, will you believe it, I thank God for you and may God forgive us."

"*Ych y fi*, don't, it could have been so unspeakable, couldn't it?"

"Will you let me away to my bed now? I'm dropping."

"Here, you didn't have your pill yet. Have you got a sheet

of paper? I'll just write 'Do not disturb' and pin it on the door."

"Paper? You're asking me for paper, after your bonfire? Are you mad as well, woman dear?"

CHAPTER 10

I needn't tell you what a mess I looked the next morning. Eyes red and swollen with all those tears, face drawn and haggard with all that sick, flesh still cringing with thoughts of Birkenhead Pringle, hands shaking with hangover, and legs and feet eaten alive with mosquito bites.

Her morning greeting was, "Jesus, have you taken a look at yourself? You look like you've had a light tap with a heavy hammer."

"Thanks. Actually I feel more like a face flannel that needs boiling, slimy with old soap and sour with old water."

"You'll never go out looking like that, sure you won't."

"Couldn't I paint my face and wear sunglasses?"

"Yes, I suppose you could, just. But I'll tell you something else, with all the carry on, you haven't a dress fit to put on you. You'll have to wear those red pants that do damn all for you. And your only clean blouse is that green one of Margaret's that we wondered why she'd ever bought."

"Oh, hell, who cares?"

"You care. I know you. You'll get miserable again if you think you look a mess."

"Get miserable? What the hell am I supposed to be now?"

"Conscience-stricken. Miserable is different. I'm having none of that sense of loss crap from you. I'm warning you."

"No, that's finished. It was mostly just a kind of bloody silly affectation, menopausal pose stuff. Everybody expecting me to react, especially Mike, so I just did. As you said, I needed my bottom warming. Maybe all I was missing was a bit of experience. God knows I've had that now.

"Despair? Good heavens, you've got to earn the right to despair. Damn, I've just remembered something. I lent one of those Americans twenty dollars last night and I didn't get it back. That's twice I've been conned, I won't let them get away with it."

"What happened last night, at all? You've been as closed as a clam on it. Come on, tell me, for a laugh."

"You'll never believe, honest; I promise you, you'll never believe. Talk about Krafft-Ebing. No more researches for me. I know it all."

"Well, go on, let's have it. Don't keep me hovering, like a fly over dung."

"Well, for a start the cocktail party was a flop. Celia never turned up, by the way. Birkenhead had a fight in the bathroom and walked out on his own party and ditched me and I was left talking to the old one, the Clay one. Oh God, it's unbelievable, that I was in it, I mean. One reads these things and one knows they happen, but it's like history or something in the books, isn't it? Well, I mean, you know the Nazis killed six million Jews but you can only count up to five on your fingers, so six million, seven million, I mean, it's meaningless, isn't it?"

"Will you tell me what happened?"

"Well this chap brought a tart in and he did that to her in front of this old chap and me. It was all supposed to be accidental – God, I can't talk about it – but they'd worked it out. Must have been when I took my bath."

"You sly bitch, fancy having a bath and not telling me."

"Yes, I enjoyed that. Got something out of it, anyway."

"But why the hell did you stay and watch? You could have walked out."

"He was holding me down. I couldn't move at first and then he said to pretend we weren't there and the other two would never know. Better not to embarrass them he said."

"Did you look?"

"Only peeped once, but I could hear. And then the young bloke hadn't the twenty dollars to pay her. Clay only had hundreds and I couldn't stand it so I gave him my money to get rid of them and, like I said, I never got it back."

"You've had that. You may kiss it goodbye. Sure, it's only money."

"No, for once money isn't only money. I'm damned if I'll pay for the privilege of living Krafft-Ebing. It's too bloody much."

"Skip it, you don't care enough about money."

"I care about this money. Twenty dollars – that's four bottles of Scotch and fifty fags over here."

"Good God, is it? Now you're talking my language. But you can't go up there to yon hotel and ask for it. Not in those red pants you can't."

"I'll give them till lunchtime to bring it back. They know where to find me and if it's not here by then I damn well will go and ask for it. Break the door down if I have to."

"Sooner you than me."

"If I get it, will you help me spend it? God knows I'll have earned it honest if I go up there."

"All right, I will. But I can't see you going. Not for money."

"Not just for money, for that money. Reach my bag and get me another tranquilliser. I've got snakes writhing in my skull and after the John Birch disclosures it's like creepy-crawlies on my loins."

"Here, take two and put it out of your mind. Guilty about the wrong things, as usual."

"Who's to say?"

"Look, why don't you just obey? It's so much easier. If you'd been a good Christian and not slept with that man you wouldn't have this class of torture now. Who the hell are you to make the rules? Ever hear of self-righteousness? That's you. Fancy yourself too much. You need humbling, so you do. If I was your priest, I'd give you. Might as well get up, I suppose. We'll be in the dog-house with the chamber-maid for that wash basin as it is. If we keep her back as well there'll be no living with her. Don't forget to leave the clothes out to be washed now and remember the dollar sweetener."

"I've just remembered one of my mother's hymns – 'Trust and obey, there is no other way to be happy in Jesus, but to trust and obey.' Used to drive me up the wall, the damn impertinence of it, the smugness. Trust whom, obey whom? Sorry, duchess, couldn't have that."

"It's just it would make your life easier," and she sang the Yeats poem "She bade me take love easy", as she got up to be first at that brown scorched wash basin.

"But you only have one life, you can't live it in a cloud of acceptance, cloud of unknowing. I am not content with this 'drawing of sufficient conclusions from insufficient premises' – Samuel Butler."

She gave me a queer glance then and crossed herself, with the hand that held her dripping face-cloth.

"Yes, I suppose you have only got one life. Let's get out of this damn room or you'll have me depressed as well. Here's a conversation to start the day. Don't you dare steal my holiday like this. Move and let me try to do something about the look of you. You're like something the cat brought in on a cold night."

That kind of crack on my appearance would, at home, have had me cringing, withering like a leaf in a blaze, wallowing in self-pity for a week, but I took it from Joan like a comment on the weather, a statement of fact. Don't ask me why.

We made our usual daily pilgrimage to the Travel Agency and got the usual daily answer. No baggage. But today they were searching in Klagenfurt. Poor Franko, we were feeling more sorry for him than for me. He was so concerned, so much was at stake, my bag was rapidly becoming symbolic of the whole Yugoslav tourist industry and I was almost ashamed to bother him. I was remarkably indifferent to the fate of my baggage by now. I kind of suspended my worry, it wasn't that I wisely decided not to worry, most of the time I didn't remember – unless I needed an excuse, like for suede at the Casino. In the same way I wasn't thinking about Mike or the kids either. About Mike's meals and the strains of the hospital and the practice and how the conference had gone and had I left enough clean socks and shirts.

A suspension. It was nice, lazy, like being in a nursing home with a very minor complaint.

On the top of my mind, of course, I had my other problems, the business of the voyeurism and Pringle's politics, but I was already seeing the funny side of the Clay thing, especially the thing, it, thimble, what have you. I think, on the whole, that women are fundamentally disloyal about sex. I gradually told Joan all the small sordid details and we cackled like Rabelaisian hens over them, and of course, we'd long since discussed our husbands and their little techniques. I'll take my oath that neither of the husbands would have done that to us. But a man is a funnier sexual object than a woman; women aren't funny laughable; devoted, intense, committed, happy but not funny pathetic. Nice to be women, nice to be secret.

No Americans had called at the hotel in our absence with twenty dollars for me and over lunch my resolution to get back my money was strengthened again. The two Germans were still with us and I tried to limit the conversation strictly to smiles, gestures and nouns. But I found it bloody irritating. A pattern had become established. A greeting, then a question about my coffer, always the same answer, "*Nein*", and always the same comment "*Ist nicht gut*". They maybe Joan would say "Concert. Beethoven" or "Mostar" and I'd say "Autobus" and they'd say "*Ja?*" and we'd nod and smile and indicate exaggerated appreciation.

I like my food, look forward to good meals and I'll happily read a cook-book even in a train, but this conversation bit put me off my feed. There's nothing more frustrating to the appreciation and digestion of food than conversation in a language you don't begin to know. And Joan was a pest too, she never seemed to remember the limitations of my German. She'd smile at them, get their attention, and then turn to me, "Tell them about so and so," she'd say. "I don't know the bloody words." "Try, go on, try, they're waiting. You'll manage." Then I'd struggle, ruin my hair-do, chew off my lipstick and then have to call the waiter to translate my terrible Italian into his shocking German. I ask you, who could take nourishment and keep good tempered in such circumstances?

By the time lunch was over that day I was good and cross again, all girded up to go and collect my just debts. Joan didn't want me to go. She kept on at me, saying "Sure, it's only money." But I'd lost those sentiments with my luggage and my innocence. Ask for money back in Cardiff? I'd rather die, but this wasn't Cardiff and it wasn't quite me. But she insisted that I sleep on it and made me lie on my bed after lunch. She quickly fell asleep, but not me, oh no, not with that temper on me. I got up very quietly and left a note on my pillow to say "Back soon". And I made my way, all sweat and snot, out of the hotel.

It was a long, uphill, hot walk from the tram terminus to their big hotel, but I went up that hill in those red pants as if I was playing for Wales.

The hotel was cool, all rubber plants and porters, but I wasn't intimidated. Hidden behind my sunglasses, I stalked across to the bank of lifts and took myself up to the room that I now knew all too well. My knock at the door was peremptory and a voice called "Come on in", but I wasn't having that. I knocked again. I'd make them open it.

Wouldn't you know it? It was old Birkenhead who came to the door and welcomed me extravagantly. "Hi, Innes, come in, come in. This is great." No apology, not a word about last night. There's a well-known cliché about taking the wind out of your sails but since I don't sail and am not a sailor left over from Trafalgar, it's not much of a metaphor for me, but I'm sure it's the relevant one for how I felt just then. When you're all armoured for a fight and the sentences are forming and – pouf – you're treated like a long-lost friend. It's disconcerting, flattening, like banging the oven door on a spongecake. The sting from your tail is perhaps a more useful metaphor, we've all in our time killed wasps. Well, anyway, that was me, windless, stingless and very hot. Red trousers and black glasses and a face like an old football boot.

Clay and young Macpherson were sitting out on the balcony in their shorts. Clay's were Black Watch, big as a marquee, and Macpherson's pale blue with starfish. They leapt to their feet and came to meet me, great welcome, extravagant joy and me in those red things and the glasses. They gave me a long, comfortable chair on the balcony and poured me a beer and said this was fun, this was great. You'd think last night had never been, that there had been no "events", no melodrama. It made me think of the silly legal use of "intimate". I'd in a sense been intimate with all three. In a slightly extended sense, I'd "known" them all sexually. But intimate? Intimate with Birkenhead? Can you commit intimacy like committing larceny? Damn people for abusing language, like terrorist because he's agin you or democrat because he's on your side. Intimate is a nice strong word, tea and sympathy stuff, it's got nothing to do with gonads and don't I know it? In fact, kissing is far more intimate than the other things, closer, more immediately near. For heaven's sake, a tongue is a far more private part.

A nice modest woman ought to be dying of shame out on that balcony where Birkenhead had carried his mattress, but I really must be awful, because I didn't give it a thought. I sat back in the long chair, crossed my long red legs and sipped my long cool beer, cold-bloodedly planning how I should now bring up the subject of my twenty dollars. Cross, I could have done it; seduced by their charm, I had to work out a new technique. When we have something to organise at home, Mike will say "Well now, let's have a general policy and then we can make a plan." My general policy remained unchanged, I'd get my money, only the plan needed a bit of adjusting.

The three men seemed all palsie-walsie again, Birkenhead back into the fold, but he was wearing long trousers and a shirt. I wondered if this was an indication that he wasn't quite in the happy family yet, but he was making free and easy with the drinks which suggested something else again. As usual he was shadowy, in the background of the conversation. I didn't exactly cut him, just gave him my effortless superiority.

I can't remember what we talked about at first, except that it was easy and comfortable in the sun. Then Macpherson said "How's about my local girlfriend, Innes? Cute little dish?"

This brought me right back, back in the bog again, "Well, I mean, I didn't see much of her, did I? No, God, I mean, I saw too much of her, but, well, oh for heaven's sake–" and of course I blushed to match my trousers and felt the sweat like beads breaking out. And they laughed at me and my floundering. Covering up, I reached over to stub out my cigarette in the ashtray on the table; too busy blushing to watch my hands, I crushed the damn thing on the edge of the tray and tipped the whole mountain of ends and ash all over the table and on to Birkenhead's sandalled feet. The other two laughed again at my confusion – nice friendly laughter, but I couldn't take laughter at me, about me, then. It gave me the jag I needed. "Actually," I said, in a *Vogue* voice, "that's why I came. You owe me twenty dollars, remember? Better make it twenty-five" I head myself say, unrehearsed, "I had to take a taxi home and they charge the earth from a posh place like this in the small hours." I couldn't believe my own ears, the cheek of it, the unlikelihood of it, the nerve.

"Yeah, I know, we got some change. We were all set to call at your place with it."

"Sorry to be a bore about it, but it is a problem of currency. Joan and I are down to dinar and we need foreign currency for Scotch and English cigarettes."

It was Macpherson himself who gave me the money and as I put it firmly into my bag, the pink of my two chips from the Casino winked at me and I praised God.

"By the way, Birkenhead, talking of currency, I owe you something, too. You staked me at the Casino and I forgot to return the stake. Here it is, two pink ones, that's right for ten white chips, isn't it? I meant to give them to you last night, but found you a little difficult to locate." It was so good to be able to pay him off in front of the others, to feel in a small way cleansed again, I can't tell you. He had the grace to look slightly discomfited by my crack about last night, but remained silent.

I threw the two pinkies on to the table, wouldn't put them in his hand, and he left them there, wouldn't pick them up.

Clay, who really was a kindly man, liking peace, snapped what was stretching between Birkenhead and me and said, "Say, why n'cher show Innes the note you got from the other chick?"

"O.K., yeah, sure," Birkenhead answered, and picked up a paper from among the drink bottles. It was from Celia, apologising for not coming to the party; she'd had a call from Siena and had had to leave. She sent me her love and said how much she'd enjoyed meeting me. And that was lovely and I felt pleased no end. But I suspect old Pringle would have kept it from me if Clay hadn't prompted him, certainly shoved it at me sourly enough, but then he did have ash in between his toes and down the sides of his sandals which couldn't have been a comfort.

I finished my beer. I had my money. It was time to go. Really time to go, to end. I looked at the three of them, took them in for the last time, and said Goodbye.

Clay held my hand and said, "Take it easy, baby, take it easy." I know that's only an American way to say Goodbye, it's like our "cheerio" which for them is only the name of a breakfast cereal, but there was a bit more to it than that too. It was a piece of advice that I could do with. Take it easy.

Birkenhead, most improbably, came with me to the door and walked me to the lift.

"Say, Innes," he said, "those two chips. Would you consider the Casino again? No point in wasting them."

Fortunately, the lift was up and I nipped in quickly and before pressing the button to close the door, I said, vulgar as they come, "Do me a favour, Pringle, go play in the traffic in a very busy street." And that, my friend, was that.

I walked more slowly down the hill, remembering Clay's "Take it easy" and I decided that I really liked Clay. All right, he'd pulled something on me, but so had I pulled something on Mike. Clay had pulled something he needed and I guess I'd needed my something too. So what? Don't let's exaggerate this one, no need for melodramatics, let's have a bit of maturity about the place. Like the man said, take it easy.

Stop a minute. Literally stop a minute and think. There's a nice wall over there and a view, islands and roofs and walls and boats. Just sit there and work this one out. Don't go back yet, the duchess is too distracting, destructive, too Irish, too mad, too wise.

O.K. So Clay was nice, we had an adventure, he taught me something and finish. Finito to that one, but it's no good hedging and avoiding the issue, and the issue is Innes and Birkenhead Pringle. That one still stands. And again, no melodramatics, please. We had those last night. We had our self-indulgence, our sick. Sick solves nothing. It was probably only the booze, anyway, dolled up to look like revulsion.

That's typical, that is, dramatise everything, even a load of vomit.

So what's the situation? I went to bed with a man who turns out to be rather unpleasant. Well, I'm not the first to do that, for a start. I'm married to a very nice man and I went to bed with a nasty one. That merely proves I'm slightly touched, that's all, heat stroke, no doubt. But, until I knew his politics stank in my nostrils, I didn't see anything wrong with it, I claimed he was only a kind of instrument and personally irrelevant. I tried to pretend that Birkenhead as Birkenhead didn't exist. The real evil is my bitchy selfishness, if I'd been in the least bit interested I could have found out about his politics; good heavens, it's my subject and I kept off it. I must have extra-sensory perceptions in my uterus that warned me off the subject. That ghost wasn't Birkenhead after all, it was probably some little man who lives in my womb who held me off from enquiring into Pringle. Because, face it, Pringle was the only contender, apart from the cinque minutis and Clay, God help him, was hardly serviceable.

As I sat on my wall working this out over a quiet fag, the old professor came up to me, carrying a string bag with bread in it and tomatoes, in his shaggy old ginger jacket and his slack, handed-down grey trousers. He munched a greeting through his slack senile lips and rested, tired against the wall. We had nothing but language in common, but he told me about London and Piccadilly Circus. I asked him to join me for a drink. I said I'd like a drink but was embarrassed to go alone and would he do me the honour. So we did that and he was glad and got me to teach him the beginning of Our Father in Welsh so that he'd know something of a Celtic language and have it to remember me by. And he and I were, for that moment, close and affectionate and that's what I mean by intimate, whatever the law has to say.

Flush with my dollars, I bought three bottles of Scotch, one for the Professor, one for the Boyds and one for us. The

Professor's delight almost made Pringle worth it. And sure, it was only money.

Joan was awake and worrying when I got back clanking with two whisky bottles.

"You did it then, you bitch. Honest, you look like a whore in those pants."

"Got it back and my taxi fare to boot. No trouble at all. Just asked for it, all ladylike and proper."

"From where, in the name of God, did you get the nerve?"

"Who cares? I got it. Sorry to be late, but I met the old professor chap and I just had to stand him a drink, God help."

"You may hurry up and get changed. You're not going down to dinner in those horrible pants. It's well Margaret's dress is black and doesn't show."

"I bought them a bottle of Scotch, look. Shall we take it to them after dinner?"

CHAPTER 11

This is a terrible chronicle of debauchery. It is by my standards, anyway, because I'm a very typical, ordinary, middle-
class wife. You might not think it, perhaps, from what I've
been telling you, but don't be hard on me, it was the holiday
that did it. If you think a minute of how I was in Yugoslavia,
suddenly on my own without Mike who's been part of me for
twenty-five years, suddenly without my clothes that are my
identity, without Wales that's my touchstone, without the
kids that are my anchor and my judge and jury.

All right, so you would have done better. How do you
know? Have you ever tried it? Tried going naked and new in
middle age? Yes, I know people have been widowed, bereft,
lost home, family, everything. I know. I know. But this is on
a different level, this is about us, the ordinary little women.
Those others are terrible tragedies, they've moved into a different dimension; let's keep this on our level, yours and mine
and Joan's. Go into a small room now and ask yourself. Tell
yourself the truth for a change, always remembering my
utterly lost luggage. I suspect you'll find you've got duck-
pond souls too; covered they are with bright, light green
water-weed, but just you wave a stick in the water and you
can expect to be prepared for anything. At least I know now
that my soul is a duck pond. It's better to know.

After the crescendo of the Americans, Joan and I settled
again to the comforting routine of sun and slivovitz, picture
postcards and cinque minuti passes, trips and tips and taxis.
We drank too much but, remember, we had to get on with
each other and neither of us was exactly accommodating.
Drink does so prune the sprouting gorge.

On one of our last mornings as we high-stepped down to
the beach we saw again the mad boy who had laughed and

burned his letter. He walked past us, fast, alone, mad, in all his formal clothes and the heat enough to drop you. We both felt now, this second time, that we must do something, offer somehow, and we spurted after him, but he went too fast, a compulsive march that took him away from us for all our hurry. We felt the guilt and responsibility – mothers ourselves.

She said, "But whatever is he doing here on his lone? Think, woman dear, if you were by yourself, like it might be you or me and you just went quietly off your rocker and nobody with you, nobody caring. Nobody but waiters and chamber-maids to take notice and them perhaps thinking it's only because you're foreign and it's none of their business. It's him being by himself that has me worried."

"Listen. I can't go any faster. I've got a stitch already. We've lost him. Don't you think the chamber-maids would sort of smell madness? We can't talk to him either, but we can see, I mean, who couldn't? I don't think he's dangerous though, do you? Except to himself. Whatever were they thinking of to let him come like this alone? But the mad are always alone, that terrible isolation, that's the worst part wouldn't you think? But whose responsibility? Somebody ought to do something. We're completely inadequate, he wouldn't thank us. But what can we do? He's so sort of symbolic, isn't he? Underlining one's personal impotence."

"There you go again. Symbolic my foot. He's just a poor wee boy's gone mad in this heat and you have to go on about personal inadequacy. Jesus, you make me sick, so you do. You try to intellectualise every damn situation you're in – honest, with you it's like doing crosswords – Here's the clue, now what's the pose?"

"D'you really think that, Joan? Am I so utterly shallow?"

"No, no, no, don't start, in the name of Jesus, Mary, Joseph and all the Saints in heaven, stop it. I didn't mean it. I wasn't thinking. He's gone now, we may give him up. At least we thought about him, we'll earn merit for that much.

"Of all the bloody awful things I've heard from you on this holiday that last takes the biscuit. We'll earn merit. We had a good thought, God, chalk it up for us, put it on our slates. Of all the reasons for wanting to help, that's even worse than doing social work to get on to a committee."

"But I had the good thought first. You won't deny that."

"No, but you've spoilt it, haven't you?"

"You are as bad as Reverend Mother, so you are. Here, it's time you carried this bag for a bit. Take it before me arm breaks."

And once again he was gone and we talked of other things and were bothered about getting a good place on the beach and being well oiled, since we both of us have these fair skins and wanted to be able to prove the holiday when we got home.

Inevitably, we went to the beach café before going to the hotel for lunch and I think it was on that same day that I rediscovered an old friend of mine. I never would have recognised him or even perhaps have remembered him again it I hadn't, carthorse that I am, fallen over his feet.

The thing was that I was reduced to those red trousers again. Anger had helped me carry them the day I'd gone to get my money back, but I had no equivalent prop this day and there was no question of adjusting my personality to those pants as there had been to Margaret's other clothes. My tarting days were over and no one in their right minds would purposely try adjusting to those pants. Pants are not for me anyway; one of my few things are my rather elegant, long legs. But there I was, God help, like a clumsy redshank on a rocky beach. I'd had to go up to the bar to order our drinks because the duchess claimed she was still incapable of saying "*uno maraschino e uno gin con aqua minerale*" in spite of all my teaching.

It had killed me to go dodging around the tables and the people in that awful get-up and I was irritable as hell, but she'd said serve me right for not getting my clothes washed. I'd worn her best bathing costume on the beach, so I wasn't really in a position to dig my heels in.

Anyway, it was me that went up to the bar. I'd put on my "look" of course, but that involves holding my head up at an uncomfortable angle so that I can appear to be looking down at the whole world over my Button B of a nose and never, never, casting a glance at the ground. I was walking back to the table and I knew everybody in the place was watching me, after all they had nothing else to do; I must have been the event of the morning. And this man was sitting there, sitting back, doing no harm to anybody, with his sandalled feet stuck out in front of him, enjoying the sun and his drink and his cigarette, and I bore down upon him, effortlessly superior, and not looking, and fell over his feet. I threw out my arms to save myself and came to rest with one hand on his table and the other on the back of his chair, embracing him, my face inches away from his, my eyes popping almost on to the glass anonymity of his sun specs, so near I felt myself squint, and my red bottom up in the air. I'd jerked the drink he'd been holding in his languid hand and it spilt all over his nice pale green silk shirt. Honestly, they ought to tie me up. I'm not safe, I promise you.

Dying, I tried to apologise and used up three whole tissues to mop up his shirt. Did I remember to say how awful Yugoslav tissues are? English and American ones – I stole a few from Clay, actually – are more precious than gold in Yugoslavia, specially if your hankies are lost in your luggage. Three tissues sound like nothing now, but there, then, they were really something. And trust me, I didn't give him the tissues; no, I kept them in my own hand and mopped his shirt myself – mother again – and him a strange man, having his nipple mopped by a lunatic female. He wasn't too pleased to have his shirt ruined, I can tell you, but I'm told I have an expressive face and he must have seen and sympa-

thised with my agony – or the mopping up was a bit ticklish
– anyway he soon laughed and said "Not to worry" in a voice
that tried but failed to be quite English. And I crept back to
the duchess who was, of course, killing herself.

I sat at our table with my back to the man and the audience
and did my monkey face, but before I'd quite finished it and
got my own face back, I felt a hand on my shoulder and he
was there again, leaning over my chair with his decimated
drink in his hand.

"Do please forgive this intrusion upon your privacy, but I
know that I have seen you before and, alas, the circumstances
escape me. And it is surely absurd – you are not the sort one
easily forgets. Tell me, where *did* we meet?" He spoke carefully, a bit pompously, a measured academic enunciation.

"She fell over your feet, remember?" Joan said, and
waving a hand with a regal gesture added, "Sit down."

"Yes, I am persuaded that I have seen you," he persisted,
dogged and academic, "but in a glass darkly – or through a
glass darkly to be more accurate and scriptural."

Actually I had remembered at once who he was, when I
looked up and saw him at our table, his slack pot was unmistakable, there at eye level. He was the man from Aberdeen
whose tie I'd recognised that first night with Birkenhead
Pringle, the night we made our first contact with American
Big Business. But I didn't think he'd want to be reminded of
that nice moment of madness. Now, in the green silk shirt
and with a suave look about him and a new sophistication, I
thought it kinder to let him forget. He'd surely be scorched
to remember. Personally I'd rather have died.

Joan was her usual, gracious, talkative self. I could have
crowned her.

"She's from Wales. Have you met her there?"

"No, I have never visited the Principality, " he said, sitting
down beside me at the table, and there was a nice male smell
of salt and sea to him. The waiter came then with our drinks

and I had to order another one for him because his own was
nearly all drying out, sweet and crinkly on his shirt, accusing
me. He told us he hailed from Aberdeen, which was no news
to me, and Joan was all intrigued about where he'd seen me
before. Was it at the symphony concert, then, or at the
Casino? No, he had unfortunately missed that concert and he
did not patronise the Casino. Fool, he was getting warmer
and warmer, soon they'd have everything eliminated and
only the restaurant would remain.

And then I saw it in his eyes. I saw him remember. He saw
me see, knew I'd known. I thought he'd die and then he
laughed and I laughed and we told her. But he couldn't leave
it there as he should have done if he'd had a proper dignity.
He tried to explain and it was painful. His shirt was too beautiful, too silken, his slacks too tapered and elegant, his
manner too precious, too academic to warrant explanations,
he should have had more sense, but we never do, do we?

He had a rational explanation handy, of course, which was
such a pity because it was his lovely, crazy irrationality
which had so delighted me that night. It was all the fault of
Scotland. He bent his head forward, like a minister collecting
his thoughts for a prayer, and then as he proceeded with his
rationalisations, he gradually brought his head up and by the
time he'd finished them he was smiling, beatific as a Buddha.
Scotland was a coffin, he claimed, and I couldn't but see all
the mourners in tartan kilts playing golf or bagpipes at the
obsequies.

He was a lecturer in classics at the university and spent his
days with texts and their emendations. As he warmed to his
self-revelations his nice, faintly Scottish accent became more
and more etiolated, he was now putting on a turn he could
have picked up in the groves of any academe.

"Once a year I get away and set about breaking every
moral law known to Marischall College and Sauchiehall
Street. I religiously get drunk on Sunday, bring disgrace on

my Aberdeen tie, spend one ritualistic night with a tart, whistle after pretty girls, never dine until nine o'clock, waste my substance, spit upon the thought of golf, and I go alone. Scotland suspects the cat that walks alone".

He needn't have said all this to us. I'm against explanations, justifications. They're hardly ever true, anyway.

It was Joan, of course, who said, "You're not married, then?"

"No. And I'm not a queer, either, speculation would be without profit." Speculating was just what she'd been up to and she blushed and laughed, confessing.

"I'm just a typical academic bachelor, not particularly active sexually, not even particularly interested. In fact I am more interested in food. Sex usually gives me such a headache, I find it so exhausting. I haven't married, I shouldn't like to set my creature comforts at risk. And what nice evil things have you two been up to? You have that smooth look of women who have triumphantly escaped."

"We've been drinking too much, for a start."

"And gambling on Sunday."

"And putting our families out of our minds."

"And sleeping in a concert."

"And not going to mass."

"And I've been unfaithful."

"Seriously unfaithful?"

"Depends what seriously means. If it means all the way, yes, if it means committed, no."

"Then we can agree, it is not serious." He was as pompously but sanely judicial now as he had been crazy and delightful on the evening of the restaurant.

"Yes, it's serious, on a different and horrible level. Because he wasn't a nice man. He turned out to be little better than a Fascist – it was a bad failure of taste. I'm not safe out alone, honestly, like a kid in the traffic. I'll have to get me to a nunnery."

"Now that would be a cardinal error, would it not, Joan?"

"No need to be blasphemous, either of you."

No need to talk like this to this man either. Talk about compulsions. Still, it might be better to get all the self-flagellations tidied up before I got back to Mike, though. I'd claimed that jealousy wasn't smart anymore, but poor old Mike was never famous for being *avant garde*, what Mike liked was comfort; me on Birkenhead Pringle would hardly be soothing.

"Not to worry." The same confident beatific smile above the shirt and the wobbly belly. "You were simply adjusting to your being alone. A nasty man was the first step away from your own nice man – for I take it that he is a nice man? After that the next step will be no man. It's like the gradual withdrawal of a drug, my dear. Not to panic."

"Balls. She's been a bad wee whore. Just you let her stew. If you eat with the pigs you may expect to stink. I've been alone too, don't you forget it. And it has been nice, I'd like to climb up into those mountains and find a big stone and hide behind it with nobody. I'd like to be naked of people for a bit longer, just to know the feel, the way a nun might long for a bath without the lid on her."

"Well, I know I can't be alone again. I'm downright wicked alone."

"But what you call wickedness has taken the form of seeking closeness, of communication. Surely that's curious? And rather a good sign?"

"Funny you should say that. Communication was exactly what I sedulously missed or perhaps deliberately avoided. How can you communicate with a fascist ghost? That's what he was, you know."

"But a séance is surely the ultimate in the search for communication, my dear child?"

"No, the ghosts in a séance are safely dead. You can't go to bed with them."

"Agreed. As for me, I rather like séances. Yes they are quite the least sexual of situations."

"Sex in a séance is like Dylan Thomas about sex at Lords, not cricket."

"But you are not seriously concerned about the infidelity, are you?" he pursued, probing away like any old gossip, all agog.

"Not about the physical act of infidelity, no. I still insist that doesn't matter at all, but it was wrong because he was wrong. He was a symbol of racist madness. No wonder he was so silent, Joan. People don't talk about their perversions. And it wasn't an obsession with him, it was a practical, political decision. *Ych y fi*! And I was wrong because, with my bloody superiority, which the duchess so justly chides me for, I wasn't prepared to consider him as a person, just a tool for my satisfaction. You disregard people at your own risk. Well, I mean, like the British in Africa, say, who couldn't tell one coloured face from another."

"Here we go again. Come on, move, I've had this and I'm hungry. Sure our place is just up the road, would you care to eat with us? Save you trekking back to the city."

"Why, that's uncommonly civil of you. Yes, thank you, I'd love that."

"Wait, though. D'you know German?"

"I can get by. Why?"

"Thank God for that. Germans at our table. He can talk to them, duchess, and I'll eat in comfort for once."

"Why ever do you call her duchess?"

"Don't know. She looks like a duchess sometimes."

We walked slowly in the lovely heat back to the hotel and he carried the beach-bag for us and there was this nice salty, male smell off him and the pine trees along the road had their smell and we had our scents and the sweetness of aperitifs on our lips and it was all kind of sensuously memorable.

When Baldo, our waiter, saw us bringing in a guest, he

pulled another table up to ours and there was lots of room and our feathered friend took over the conversation. For me it was like taking off my shoes and my corset and the combs out of my hair. I made no effort to follow what they were saying, his German seemed much more than adequate and he was throwing himself in the role, with his usual histrionic exaggeration. I quietly opted out. But Joan fed Luke – that was the Aberdonian's name – she fed him bits of information and suggested topics as she felt the need arose. I thought I heard him say something like Herzog a few times and Herzogin and thought they were having an intellectual discussion about modern American novels, which rather surprised me. I'd put the German down for an engineer. No English nor any other foreign language? That was surprising enough, but a knowledge of modern Americana? Very odd.

The Germans were leaving that day and stood us a bottle of champagne and then Luke stood us another one, wasting his substance. They took farewell pictures of us at the table and thanks to the bubbly I only hid behind sunglasses from the camera. The red pants were safely under the table cloth. I noticed a certain kind of humility in the nice little Frau's attitude to us, a kind of obsequiousness that I put down to German sentimentality because it was goodbye. We walked with them to their car and waved madly and then retired, exhausted, to sit under the trees in the hotel garden.

Luke was still being his flamboyant German self. His prissy manner was all gone now and he was looking particularly chuffed. He had a glint in his eye that was more than champagne and was obviously having a secret giggle over something.

"Thank you for that," I said to him, flopping into a deckchair that promptly broke under my weight. While he fussed setting up another one and Joan hauled me to my feet, I went on, "That last lunch would have been torture without you. Inspired idea to ask him, duchess."

"Aye, sure I'm full of good ideas. What about a brandy now?"

"Great. You had a fearfully intellectual conversation, didn't you, Luke? I wouldn't have expected them to be Saul Bellow addicts."

"Saul Bellow, dear?"

"I'm sure I heard you talk about Herzog, the Bellow novel?"

Then he seemed to shrivel up on himself and let out a high-pitched giggle. He flapped his hands and drummed his heels and was convulsed. He choked on his giggles and Joan had to bang his back till his black forelock bounced on his brow and his eyes bulged, swimming; when his breath came back he laughed again and his slack little pot was heaving; he looked like old Selinus.

"Oh, no," he said, at last, "Saul Bellow. It's priceless."

"Will you not tell us the joke, man dear? You're killing us."

"Darlings, Herzog is German for duke, Herzogin is duchess. I told our German friends that you were the Duchess of Connemara travelling incognito and that Innes was the Baroness of Glamorgan. My dear, I made their holiday."

"No wonder they had us signing yon menu card. Are you mad at all?"

"And who were you in this fantasy? What right had you to be hobnobbing with duchesses and baronesses?"

"But I am the duchess's devoted admirer, without wealth or title, who flew out to reassure myself that all was well with her."

Our brandies came and we solemnly toasted each other in our new titles and laughed like fiends.

He left us, to pack for the night flight to Edinburgh, and we went to sleep off the lunch and were glad we'd found him.

That evening there was a new influx of guests in the hotel and two fat girls from the Midlands shared our table. We almost regretted the Germans.

The departure of the Germans shifted us into a new gear.

After that we moved a bit apart. We were, for example indifferent to each other's choice of presents for the young and the husbands, we began to have separate finances, we checked that our tickets were safe for our separate journeys.

When we were writing last-minute duty cards to mothers-in-law and neighbours and the wives of husbands' colleagues, we knew that it was over, that we were willingly reverting to duty, to the tracks, the round; the comforts of the commonplace.

We were on the beach and the last of the sun, of the sea, and it was like the final minutes in bed after the alarm has gone off. She looked up from the cards. "You'll write to me, won't you?"

"No, duchess, I won't."

"And why ever not?"

"Don't be daft now. We only belong here. It wouldn't work in Ballyduggan and Cardiff. Use your head, good girl."

"What harm in writing, keeping in touch?"

"We'll be lovely subjects to dine out on, dearie, let's keep it like that. Keep it sweet. Don't get sentimental. It's not our style."

"Christ knows you're a bitch, Innes Gibson. You're treating me like that letter you wrote. Burnt in a sink to stoke a pair of polluted pants, that's me."

"Better that than slow disintegration in a dustbin. Have a bit of sense, duchess, we don't fit anywhere but here. Things are fraying already between us. We've had a holiday romance. Think of the husbands trying to get on, for a start."

"All right, you do have a bit of sense the odd time, mad as you are. So we'll send Christmas cards and the births, marriages and deaths, right?

"Right. Remind them to inform me of your death because of the brown shroud and purple flowers. I'll be faithful in my fashion."

Back at the hotel, I took our pile of cards to the post-box in the foyer while Joan collected our key. I ran over them to check addresses and stamps, you know the way you do, and when I joined her again she was holding an unopened telegram in her hand, turning it round and round, stupefied, without the courage to open it.

"What is it," I said, "What's the matter?"

"A telegram. Oh God, it's my children, I know it is."

"Here, give it to me. Can't be the children, it's addressed to both of us, idiot." I snatched it from her, and tore it open. The message was "Fear aliases penetrated cover broken suggest flee instanter Awellw Isher". I'd hardly finished reading it and hadn't begun to understand it when I felt a big shadow looming over me and a voice said "Madam Maguire, Madam Gibson?" and there were these two policemen standing beside us, guns, hats, all the trimmings. I'm terrified of policemen, anyway, and for Joan, a Roman Catholic in Northern Ireland, they spelt the Special Powers Act, imprisonment on suspicion and the Crumlin Road Jail. But there's something in me that refuses to be brow-beaten by a gun. I put on my look.

"I am Mrs Gibson. Can I help you?"

"The telegram, madam, we would like please some explanations. You will be good enough to explain, please?"

"*Gospod*, if you will give me time to read it, I might conceivably make sense of it."

"Your passaporta, please?"

"Our passports are in our room, *drug*. Joan, love, nip up and get them. Relax, for God's sake, woman. We haven't done anything. Stop looking so damn scared or they'll have us in jail on suspicion. Madam Maguire will collect our passports." She gave me a look like a frightened rabbit, all teeth and eyes, and she slowly mounted the stairs, followed closely by the hotel manager and by the second policeman. She dragged up the stairs, trailing her hand on the rail, like a small girl sent to bed.

I studied the damn telegram again. No wonder the police had been alerted, aliases and covers and who the hell was Awellw Isher? Sounded Nigerian, but the only Nigerian in my repertoire was in jail, in England. The post office must have made a mistake and sent us someone else's telegram. I was scared rotten, but I was damned if I'd show. The policeman was impatient, tapping his foot on the ground and playing chopsticks on the reception desk. But he was still being very polite, there was no show of force, only the gun in its holster and the hat firmly on his head and the whole terrifying thing of a uniform.

"I can make no sense of this, I am afraid. It is a mistake at the post office. But I can sympathise with your suspicions, *gospod*. It is quite meaningless to me, I do assure you." He took it from my shivering, lifeless, over-ringed hand.

"But your names, madam, and this hotel. The post office makes no mistake. This message is for you. That much is clear. It is difficult to believe it means nothing, is that not so?"

"Very difficult. I do so agree, *gospod*. We must think. Do not permit yourself to rush into hasty conclusions. I am persuaded that you would not wish to begin an international incident?" Panicking, I found my diction turning nineteenth century, maybe I was thinking in gun-boat terms; Disraeli, thou should'st be living at this hour. I knew in my guts that it wasn't really a post-office mistake. There had to be a rational explanation. But Awellw Isher? Wait, could there be a small mistake after all? Who knew, apart from the families, that we were here together?

"Wait now, wait a minute. I've had a thought. What is the place of origin? Where does it come from? It wouldn't be Aberdeen, would it?"

"Place of origin? It comes from? Yes, Aberdeen. It is in United Kingdom, no?"

"Now I understand. It is a joke. Look, I'll show you. The signature should be A Well-wisher – one who wishes you well, you see? This is from a man who was here, in this hotel, for lunch a few days ago, the waiter will tell you. He is a man who likes to make a joke. Do you understand? He makes such a joke because he pretended that we were titled ladies, of the English aristocracy. And it is a joke because we are good socialists, *drug*. Here he says 'aliases' because we are not aristocratic, because we do not like the aristocrats. So he makes this joke. To make us laugh, you see?"

"No, I am not sure. You leave this country when?"

"Tomorrow. It will be sad for us. We love your country."

Joan came cringing down the stairs and he rounded on her, "What do you know of Aberdeen?" he demanded, hectoring before I could get a word in.

"Aberdeen?" The fear fell from her face, it was like wiping off a mud pack. "Och, it's from that lunatic. Oh, the fright he gave me. I'll have his life, so I will."

"What is about Aberdeen, madam?"

"Well, sure, it was this fellow we met. She fell over his feet and we brought him in here and gave him lunch and didn't he pretend I was a duchess and her a baroness and sure we're no more titled than you are yourself, man. Och, I need a drink. Come on, man dear, what'll you have and no hard feelings? A wee brandy now to help you on?"

I felt for the policeman. He looked as bewildered as Franko had done when she threatened to take his trousers down. But her obvious relief had shaken him, weakened him. He took our passports from her and could find nothing wrong with them, little did he know about me travelling on Mike's passport. His confident, policeman's style evaporated in the sun of Joan's beauty and her suddenly restored good humour. He looked as if he wasn't sure what had walloped him. She proceeded to order brandies, for him and for his colleague, for the manager, the receptionist and for us. She sat down at the foyer table as though holding court and the drinks were there and what could they do but drink them?

"Sit down, man dear," she said to the first policeman. "Take the weight off your feet and take off that hat of yours. It puts me off, so it does. Here's to you and may all your enemies be confounded." Slowly the policeman bent himself into a chair and took off his hat and his head was bald and beaded with sweat and the red mark of the hat around his crown. His subordinate remained standing, rigid, ungiving.

My guts were still churning and I was having the flush of a life-time. My knees wouldn't let me walk over to the table. I leaned against the reception desk, almost praying aloud. I had to have a fag. I dived into my handbag to find one and the other policeman was immediately at my side, alert as a terrier. My bag was, I suppose, big enough to be holding a gun, but really, I mean, how melodramatic can you get? I handed him my bag and said *"Uno cigarette, per favore, drug?"* He had the grace to look daft and gave the bag back to me and I offered him the pack but he shook his head. Baldo brought my brandy over to me and I in turn handed it to my policeman.

"Fino, per favore." Hesitating, he looked across at his superior, wondered where promotion lay, and then he knocked the brandy back and struck a match for the cigarette I was still feverishly fingering.

And that was how we came to have the most enjoyable lunch with two charming policemen and no *cinque minutis* either. But they kept our telegram. I wonder if we have a dossier apiece by now.

There had to be a last visit to Franko and on that last day he said "Today they search in Ankara" which I thought was wonderful.

"And tomorrow, Franko, where tomorrow?"

"We hear there is a *coffer* not claimed in Prague. Perhaps it comes, who knows?"

I wrote him a letter when I got home, to say my bag had been all the time in London Airport and that the Yugoslav Tourist organisation had been in no way to blame. I thanked him for all his trouble over me, but he didn't answer my letter. I hope he hasn't done anything foolish again, Bosnian boy that he was.

We had dinner with the Boyds on our last night. Gloved and hatted and suited for the plan, it was like having a meal in a strange railway station between trains. The train we knew had gone, with our newspapers and fag ends and paper cups and temporary ownership, and we waited for another train that was the end of escape and the promise of –

I returned the clothes to Margaret and said the usual things, and for her and for Alan they were just some clothes she'd let me borrow and I let it ride. Like the tart in the hotel, she'll never know

The duchess and I went our separate ways at the Yugoslav airport. She to fly to Dublin, me to London. One of the last things she said to me was, "I wonder what you'll tell your man."

"I shall give him an edited account, duchess, don't we always?"

MORE GREAT NOVELS FROM MENNA GALLIE

You're Welcome to Ulster

Introduction by Claire Connolly and Angela V. John

First published in 1970, this was one of the very first novels to confront The Troubles in Northern Ireland. This compelling story also reflects the bid for sexual freedom of the late 1960s.

Sarah Thomas has a life-threatening illness and decides that it is time for what might be her last holiday and opportunity to revisit old friends and a lover in Ulster.

Unwittingly her visit coincides with the Twelfth of July. From the moment she drives off in her hired Mini, Sarah becomes entwined with the deepening political crisis that is enveloping Northern Ireland and even impinging on her native Wales.

You're Welcome to Ulster brings a uniquely Welsh perspective to the unfolding tragedy and its causes and is written with Menna Gallie's customary wit, verve and insight.

£8.99
978-1-906784-19-5

Strike for a Kingdom

Introduction by Angela V. John

First published in 1959, this novel is set in the fictional Valleys town of Cilhendre at the time of the 1926 miners' strike. The murder of a hated mine manager exposes the tensions and secrets of this close knit South Wales community. The book was described by critics at the time as an 'outstanding detective story that is genuinely different' and as a 'poet's novel' despite being a 'whodunnit'. *Strike for a Kingdom* was shortlisted for the CWA Gold Dagger Award.

£8.99
978-1-906784-20-1

The Small Mine

Introduction by Jane Aaron

First published in 1962, this novel tells the tale of a young collier's death in a mining accident in Cilhendre, a fictional village in the South Wales valleys. It vividly and sympathetically portrays how the Valley community, and in particular its women, struggles to come to terms with sudden loss – an occurrence with which it is all too familiar.

Yuri Gagarin has made the first trip into space (1961) but small mines are still in operation and privately owned. Joe leaves his job with the Coal Board and goes to work in one such small mine for more pay but with much worse conditions. He pays a high price for his higher wage – meeting with a sudden death by industrial accident. An inquest into the cause of the accident and Joe's death closes the mine on grounds of negligence, but the villagers are suspicious and point the finger not at an accident but at Link, a local who lost his job…

£8.99
978-1-906784-21-8

All Honno titles are available from good bookstores
and online booksellers.
They can also be ordered online at **www.honno.co.uk**,
with **free** p&p to all UK addresses.

MORE GREAT CLASSICS FROM HONNO

Honno's Classics are a unique series which bring books by women writers from Wales, long since out of print, to a new generation of readers.

Dew on the Grass
Eiluned Lewis
With a new explanatory introduction by Dr Katie Gramich.
Set in the Welsh borders, this enchanting autobiographical novel vividly evokes the essence of childhood and a vanished way of life. The novel was first published in 1934 to great acclaim.
9781870206808 £8.99

Stranger Within the Gates
Bertha Thomas
Edited by Kirsti Bohata
A collection of witty, sharply observed short stories written at a time of great social change, when the fundamental rights of women were being questioned. Bertha Thomas deftly sketches her characters with a keen eye for satirical details.
9781870206945 £8.99

A View Across the Valley: Short Stories by Women from Wales c. 1850 – 1950
Edited by Jane Aaron
Stories reflecting the realities, dreams and personal images of Wales – from the industrial communities of the south to the hinterlands of the rural west. This rich and diverse collection discovers a lost tradition of English-language short story writing.
9781870206358 £7.95

Queen of the Rushes: A Tale of the Welsh Revival
Allen Raine
First published in 1906 and set at the time of the 1904 Revival. An enthralling tale of complex lives and loves, it will capture the romantic heart of any modern reader.
9781870206297 £7.95

All Honno titles are available from good bookstores and online booksellers.
They can also be ordered online at **www.honno.co.uk**, with **free** p&p to all UK addresses.

ABOUT HONNO

Honno Welsh Women's Press was set up in 1986 by a group of women who felt strongly that women in Wales needed wider opportunities to see their writing in print and to become involved in the publishing process. Our aim is to develop the writing talents of women in Wales, give them new and exciting opportunities to see their work published and often to give them their first 'break' as a writer.

Honno is registered as a community co-operative. Any profit that Honno makes is invested in the publishing programme. Women from Wales and around the world have expressed their support for Honno by buying shares. Supporters liability is limited to the amount invested and each supporter has a vote at the Annual General Meeting.

To buy shares or to receive further information about forthcoming publications, please write to Honno at the address below, or visit our website: www.honno.co.uk.

Honno
Unit 14, Creative Units
Aberystwyth Arts Centre
Penglais Campus
Aberystwyth
Ceredigion
SY23 3GL

All Honno titles can be ordered online at
www.honno.co.uk
or by sending a cheque to Honno.
Free p&p to all UK addresses